The Mouse That Meowed

A Seymour Story

Alfred J. Walker

Illustrated by Dennis Yap

ISBN 151870249X
ISBN 13: 9781518702495
Library of Congress Control Number: 2016902800
CreateSpace Independent Publishing Platform
North Charleston, South Carolina

For Heather, my wife, my partner and a great editor

Chapter 1

Melissa in Trouble

It should not have happened like this, it should not have happened at all, but it did.

Melissa was outside. The grass in the field was high enough to cover most of her, so she felt sufficiently safe that she was hidden from view of any other animals, and people. The large field was one of her favorite places to be, other than up in the barn, and what better place than here in the grass with the late morning sun splashing over her, providing the warmth that was so welcome. She was centered on events of the past few days, and every few seconds she stopped and listened to the sounds of nature. What was most important was hearing the noises of the birds that, acting as an early defense team, could be counted upon to give a cry at the first sign of danger. Melissa knew that hawks often circled in the sky, on the lookout for smaller animals like mice or chipmunks, or even the birds themselves, to eat. Now, their chattering signaled to her that there were no predators nearby. The barn was only a few yards from where she crouched and, as she had been trained to do, she kept an eye on her surroundings. Seeing no prowling cats, or horses that might inadvertently step on her, she moved further into the field.

As noon approached, so preoccupied with her thoughts, so lulled by the nearness of home and the lazy warmth of the sun, Melissa was stunned to suddenly find herself lifted off the ground! She cried out for help, but it happened so fast she had no chance of escape. Was a hawk taking her? Was it a cat? Was she to be eaten? Then, suddenly, she was thrust into darkness. She screamed and screamed, but a heavy fabric that now enfolded her muffled her sounds.

As Melissa struggled to subdue her fear and gather her senses, she took a deep breath and realized that she was being carried in a bag of some sort. She was bouncing so much that, try as she might, she could not grasp the sides of the sack and climb out. She heard heavy footsteps, and it came to her that it was a human who had her, not an animal. An animal, like a cat or a coyote or a fox, would have eaten her by now, not put her in a bag! After what seemed like a very long time, the sack stopped shaking and she heard the sounds of doors opening and closing and humans talking.

"We will put the mouse in a cage, but first we have to find out if it is a sound specimen, what its age is, and whether it is male or female," a human voice said. "Next, we have to examine its markings so we will be able to identify it again. So we must be careful not to harm it. Are my instructions clear?"

"Yes, Doctor, they are clear," said another voice. "How will we do these things?"

"Watch me, Mrs. Bennett."

"But what if it's not a sound mouse? What do we do with it then?"

"What do I care," the male voice said gruffly, "throw it into the yard or in the garbage. What I must have for the Program are good, clean, sound mice. Do you understand me?"

"Yes, Doctor."

Melissa, of course, had no idea what these humans were saying, but their voices frightened her more than anything she had ever heard in her life. Before she knew what was happening, she was turned upside down and dropped out of the bag onto a table, making a small thump. The moment she hit the table her instincts told her to run! She tried to scamper away, but one of the humans grabbed her by the tail and lifted her into the air. She wiggled and twisted and tried to get free but she could not. A man in a white coat was holding her in front of his face and staring at her through black-rimmed glasses. Nearby, she saw the other person to whom the man was talking, a woman, standing next to him.

"Turn on the tape recorder," the man ordered.

Melissa saw the woman move to another table, where there were cages of all different sizes and several devices with wires coming in and out of them. The woman turned a knob on one of the machines, and little yellow and green lights on the device came alive. Then she picked up another black plastic thing and brought it to the table where the man was standing. Melissa was still being held in the air by her tail, a painful position she did not like at all, and she continued to jerk her body this way and that, trying to get free. The man was looking closely at her and his intensity made Melissa feel very creepy.

"What we have here," the man said into the microphone the woman had given him, "is a female field mouse approximately two years of age. She is lively, bright, and appears to be in good physical condition. She has a light brown coat and a white throat and chest. I will put her in a cage now, and we will see if she eats and drinks. If she does, and continues to show positive signs in captivity, we will enter her into the program as Mouse #16." Though she couldn't understand a word, every sound the man made caused shivers to run up Melissa's spine.

The man walked over to a cage, opened the door, and pushed Melissa inside, locking the door.

Chapter 2

Brainwashing Begins

As she watched them walk away from her cage, Melissa was feeling as alone and afraid as she had ever been. Where was she and why was she in such a strange place, in a box with wire sides? She had no idea who the two people were or what they were saying. The only human speech she had ever heard was when Mr. Saunders came down to the barn to feed the horses, and she could not understand the sounds he made.

Turning around, Melissa saw that there was water and some grain in her cage, and wood shavings on the floor. She was not hungry or thirsty though; she was way too scared. Looking out into the room, she saw the table where she had been examined, some chairs and overhead lights, and the other table where the machines were kept. That was the extent of the furniture in the room. There were two high windows, one on each side of the room, and through them some light shone in. But nothing looked familiar. So where was she?

As the time passed, the exhausted mouse lay down and closed her eyes, and slept. When she awoke, she explored the cage but found no way out; the spaces between the sides were just too small to squeeze through. And trying to chew through the cage proved hopeless; her tiny mouse teeth would not cut through metal. Looking up, she saw that there was no longer any light coming through the windows, so she knew it was nighttime. She finally ate a few bits of grain and drank a sip or two of water and, still suffering the aftereffects of shock, she fell back asleep.

Mice are nocturnal animals, so Melissa was awake a good bit during the night. She had never been all alone before, away from the barn and her family. Frightened to the core and unaccustomed to the confinement of a cage, the only thought running through her head was escape. Unable to get into a quiet or relaxed state, she paced around the cage what seemed like hundreds of times.

Melissa was awake and pacing when the door opened and the man walked in, with the woman right behind him. "All right mouse, let's see how you are this morning," said the man as he came up to the cage. "So, you have eaten a bit and taken some water. Good, good. Those are very good indications. You are a good mouse, which is exactly what we want, isn't it?"

He turned his head and spoke to the woman. "Mrs. Bennet, prepare the table for our guest, would you? And let's get some Scopolamine ready as well. Is the electrical persuader hooked up?" And, again turning to Melissa, he said, "Mouse, your training program is about to begin."

Melissa had no idea what was being said or what was about to happen, but the look on the man's face and the tone of his voice alarmed her more than ever. He opened the cage door and reached in for her, and Melissa backed up as far as she could and then darted past his hand, trying to get to the open door. But the man was clearly no stranger to retrieving small animals from their cages. In her panic, Melissa ran right into a net that he had positioned at the cage door. If she had moved more slowly, she might have seen the net and avoided it, but that was not the case. She was caught, and before she could get her wits about her, she was back on the table in the center of the room, being held down by both the man and the woman. Melissa took a deep breath and squealed and cried as loud as she could.

"Tape, please," the man commanded. The woman tore off a few inches of adhesive tape and handed it to the man, who taped one of

Melissa's forelegs to the table. Then her other legs were taped down, one by one, so that in just a few seconds the mouse was spread-eagled on her back, unable to move.

"There, mouse, that wasn't so bad, was it? Listen to this, if you would." The man reached over and turned on a voice recorder he had positioned on the table.

What Melissa heard was a mouse talking in her native mouse dialect. "Calm down, Sister, you will be fine," the recorder played. "You are in a laboratory under the care of one of the finest doctors in the world. You will not be hurt, you will be cured of any illness that you might have, and you will be better than ever. That is why you are here."

Melissa was bewildered. Although she could not move her arms or legs, she was able to turn her head, and she looked at the recorder. She had never heard anything like this before, a female mouse's voice but no mouse nearby making the sounds. In the barn where she lived, her uncle Seymour had a laptop computer, an iPhone, printers and other equipment, but they did not make mouse language. She did not understand this machine. How did it work? Was there a mouse inside it? She was as scared as ever, even though the voice was telling her to be calm.

"You are here, as I said before, to let us help you," said the mouse voice. "We will make you better than you have ever been. These humans know more about medical things than we mice do. They have medicines and other machines that no one else has, and they will make you a smarter and wiser mouse. You agree that will help, don't you? You want to be the best mouse you can be, and I know that in time you will come to understand more fully what I am saying. So relax, if you can, the doctor will give you some medicine now to help you get better. Just lay there and relax."

So the man was a doctor. An animal doctor had treated Melissa some months ago when she had stomach problems, fever, and the sniffles. But doctors were good! Why was this man being so mean to her?

The doctor approached Melissa and, swiftly putting something cold on her skin that made it feel funny, he injected a small amount of substance into her. "There we are, mouse," he said. "That wasn't painful,

"… the mouse was spread-eagled on her back unable to move."

was it? I administered some numbing gel on your side so that the needle wouldn't hurt. Now let's give this medicine a minute or two to work, and then we will continue with the program. The medicine should help you concentrate on what we are about to tell you, and help you remember it. This electricity will also help you forget some of the things we want you to forget."

Melissa felt wires being clipped onto her head, and though she twisted and turned to avoid them, the tape held her down. The drug she was given made her feel drowsy, then calm, and there now seemed to be a rosy colored glare to the lights. She was not prepared for the electric shock that suddenly jolted her small body and might have lifted her off the table if she hadn't been fastened to it. It hurt. What was happening? Melissa screamed as loud as she could.

Just then the voice on the recorder started again. "Please, Sister, do not cry, this will help you and make you a better mouse. Please listen to me. There is nothing to be afraid of. There are no enemies here, nothing to harm you. The doctor and Mrs. Bennett are here to help you to be a more accepting and wise mouse, a mouse that knows that she will be the best mouse in the world. You will come to see and understand that other animals, such as cats, are not in the world to harm us. They are superior to mice, yes, I know it may be hard for you to believe it, but they are. However, this is why you are here: you can become a cat yourself. Yes, you can! After just a day or two of this training, you will know that, not only are cats harmless to mice, you will see yourself as a cat if you do well in the program – you will in fact join them and become a cat." Then another shock coursed through Melissa's body and she passed out.

Melissa did not know exactly how long she was in the laboratory, but she knew the training went on for days because she noticed the sunlight appear or disappear as she watched from her cage. She was taken to the table many times, and each session involved an injection of a powerful drug, and electric shock treatment. During those sessions, the voice recordings droned on in her head, telling her that she would no longer be a mouse, but a cat. In time, she came to look forward to the sessions. And eventually, Melissa began forgetting parts of her past.

Finally, the small mouse was taken out of her cage and landed a backpack with a tiny recorder in it and some other materials. She walked unaided to the table and climbed onto it, no longer needing to be strapped down. Mrs. Bennett turned on the recorder and Melissa heard the voice. "Well, what we have here is a cat, not a mouse. You may look like a mouse, but you are no longer a mouse on the inside. You are a cat. Mrs. Bennett will be your Master, and she will guide you from now on.

"Now return to your home. Mrs. Bennett's house is just a short walk from your barn, and she will show you the way back to it. Every night when the sun goes down, go to your Master's house. There you will meet other mice such as yourself and your training will continue.

"Remember, Mrs. Bennett will be your Master and you will do what she says without fail. From time to time she will give you lessons, which you must be sure to learn. She will show you nice pictures of cats to remind you of just how beautiful cats are. Go with her now."

With that, Melissa was brought out to the driveway and she walked back to her barn, with Mrs. Bennett showing her the way.

Chapter 3

Seymour Is Perplexed

"No, the cats will not kill you if you go down there," said Melissa, who overheard a comment her friend Harold had made. "Cats are good, not bad, and they will not eat mice."

Melissa's remarkable statement, delivered in a strangely sleepy sounding voice, drew Seymour's attention immediately. He knew that just the opposite was true, that cats were not necessarily evil animals, but they did indeed kill and eat mice. He had always instructed the mice to be as careful as they could when they ventured out of the hayloft. This was especially true where cats were concerned. They were very accomplished hunters and mice needed to avoid them at all costs. In discussions of this sort he told the mice that while cats were given food in a dish every day on the ground floor of the barn and did not need to supplement their diet by eating mice, they would if they had the opportunity – that's just how cats are.

Seymour lived with his nieces and nephews in a horse barn in the country where they were very comfortable, staying safely within the walls and living on grain, corn, and feed dropped by the horses. Arguably the most famous mouse in the world, Seymour had been responsible for many daring rescues, and performed heroic deeds for mayors, governors and even the President of the United States. He had unique capabilities:

he could understand and communicate with humans as well as with mice as he knew mouse language and English. He could read write, operate his laptop and cell phone, as well as drive a vehicle, a used school bus. In other words, he was a very special mouse.

It was a typical summer day, sunny and warm. Up in the hayloft the mice were running around as they normally did, creating a lot of noise and general havoc. At the moment, they were playing the "hide the cheese game". Cheese was a rare treat for the mice; they found a few tiny chunks near the horses' stalls on occasion, left there for the mice by the benevolent Mr. Saunders. The mice covered their eyes and ears while one of them hid a piece of cheese, and whichever mouse found it first got to eat it. The lucky mouse then assumed the role of the "hider". This was one of their favorite games and it always continued until they ran out of cheese.

Seymour had returned to the barn late the night before after a week's trip to Europe, where he had been successful in assisting the Spanish government stopping ruthless men from another country steal some of Spain's most precious resources. Due to this absence, he was unaware that Melissa had been missing for a few days. He was used to the semi-controlled mayhem around him and was filing some papers at his desk when he overheard Harold tell Jeffrey, another mouse to be careful not to drop the cheese down the hay door in the floor. And he was quite surprised to hear Melissa's response about the cats.

"Melissa," Seymour called, "would you come here for a moment, please."

"What is it, Seymour?" Melissa asked as she stepped up to Seymour's desk.

Before answering her, Seymour said sternly, "Mice, quiet … please! I am trying to talk to Melissa." Then, turning to Melissa, he asked, "What did I just hear you say about cats being good, and that they would not eat mice?"

"It's true Seymour," Melissa replied. "Cats are the best animals in the world! They are kind, gentle, furry creatures that love everyone and hurt no one, not even mice." Again, Seymour noted that Melissa's voice had an odd tone.

"Melissa, you know I love all animals, even one or two cats, but you must not think for a moment that they would not kill and eat a mouse if they had a chance. Why, even our own barn cat, little Seek, might stalk and pounce on one of us before we had a chance to hide. Now please do not tell any of the other mice that they shouldn't fear cats. They should, they must always beware of cats. They are, without exception, our most dangerous enemy."

Melissa bristled at Seymour's description of cats and their demeanor, but not wanting to argue with Seymour at this time, she said, "Okay Seymour, I'll go rejoin the game now," and she walked away.

Seymour sat for a few minutes reflecting on the short conversation he'd just had with Melissa. He did not like it one bit but he did not know what to make of it either. He had work to do, so he turned back to his desk and continued filing his papers, and when that was accomplished he went on to respond to e-mails and pay some bills.

Later that morning, however, Seymour was interrupted by a commotion coming from the other side of the hayloft. He was on the phone with the Governor of New Jersey regarding the Governor's request to help out at an upcoming fund raising event at a local hospital, when he heard Melissa again. This time, she was shouting at the mice. "Stop squeaking! I hate squeaking! It's so, so … mouse! Squeaking is bad," she said, and her voice changed as she continued, "Purring is good. Learn to purrrrrr like cats. Purrrrring is much better than squeaking." As he listened, Seymour realized there obviously was something very strange going on. His niece, a mouse, sounded like … a cat!

This was too much for Seymour. He excused himself with the Governor and promised to call him back. He went to Melissa, gently took her by the hand and asked what was going on, why was she saying that squeaking was bad? "That's what mice do," Seymour explained. "You should know that Melissa," he went on "you're a mouse yourself."

"Well, you may think so Seymour. You may see me as a mouse, but I prefer cats to all other animals or even humans, and I would rather be a cat than a mouse. In fact, I believe I am a cat."

Seymour touched Melissa's forehead, asked her if she felt alright or did she feel faint? Did she have an illness? Did she pick up some germs while he was gone? No, she said, she felt very well, thank you very much. She stood as tall as she could and, looking straight at Seymour with fire in her eyes, Melissa stated, "I _am_ a cat!"

Chapter 4

Seymour Consults Mr. Saunders

Seymour knew something was really amiss here, but decided it was best not to debate the issue at this time. Melissa was becoming very difficult to deal with and he thought that perhaps a short nap would help her, and maybe after that she would come to her senses. When he led her to her little sleeping area in the corner of the hayloft, he was astounded at what he saw. There were pictures of cats tacked on the walls and ceiling all around Melissa's nest. There were easily two dozen pictures hanging there, big cats, little cats, older cats and kittens. He saw Persians, Siamese, Manx and Abyssinians, and those were just the ones Seymour could identify.

"Melissa," Seymour implored, "what is this? Where did you get these pictures, and why are they here?"

"Aren't they just so dear, Seymour?" Melissa sighed. "I don't know exactly where I got them, perhaps from magazines and newspapers, it doesn't matter. I like looking at them, Seymour. I think of them as my family now."

"Melissa, <u>we</u> are your family and have been since you were born!" cried Seymour. "What is going on here?"

"... *pictures of cats tacked on the walls and ceiling all around Melissa's ne*

"Nothing is 'going on' Seymour, I am fine here with my pictures. But I am a bit hungry. Could you perhaps get me some tuna fish or Meow-Mix?"

Seymour was flabbergasted, and he had no idea what to do with Melissa. It appeared that she was living in some fantasyland where cats were the perfect creatures. Melissa was one of the most trustworthy mice in the barn, and when he was called on to leave the barn to help on a mission, she was usually one of the mice he put in charge. But now, she was clearly not in her right mind. Not her normal self. It was a dangerous state to be in because she *was a mouse*. Her belief that cats would not harm her was wrong, dead wrong. Seymour told her to take a nap and he would look into the food issue later.

Seymour then went up to the house to talk to Mr. Theodore Saunders, the owner of the house and barn. They were very good friends, and Seymour needed someone's perspective about what had just happened with Melissa. He knocked on the back door, and called out, "Mr. Saunders, can I talk to you for a few minutes?"

"Certainly Seymour, come on in," said Mr. Saunders. "I always have time for you. What's up?"

Mr. Saunders was a tall, soft-spoken gentleman who, although now retired, had served as a professor at Rutgers University and was a very good listener. He knew all about Seymour's special capabilities and helped whenever he could. He was drinking his morning coffee and reading the newspaper. "Come on, pull up a chair and tell me what's on your mind."

Seymour jumped up on a chair and sat down.

"Well, it seems that we might have a problem with one of the mice. It's Melissa," said Seymour.

"I know Melissa, what's wrong with her, Seymour? Is she sick, or hurt? Does she need a vet?"

"I'm not sure what's wrong, Sir." Seymour related the events that had just taken place and the conversation he had with Melissa. "I've never seen her, or any of the mice, behave that way before. They know enough to keep away from cats. They were raised that way, and we have seen firsthand how dangerous they can be." Seymour was referring to an incident where one of the barn mice, Larry by name, had led another mouse to the cats in exchange for a promise of cheese. It had not turned out well for either of those mice.

"It's an interesting problem, Seymour. I have a few questions. For example, where did she get the cat posters? There were certainly none of those in the barn."

"Good question," replied Seymour. "I asked Melissa, but she did not seem to know. She said maybe from a magazine or a newspaper."

"Hmm. It was a good answer for her to give, but perhaps too quick a response from what you asked her. No, I don't think she did this by herself, Seymour. Where would Melissa find magazines or newspapers, and why would she search for cat pictures? That's one problem. Then there is the issue of cutting them out," Saunders continued. "Where did she get a knife or scissors, and given her size, how could she use them?"

"There are scissors in the barn, Mr. Saunders. You and others need them to cut the twine on the hay bales."

"True, they are there. However, could she carry them up to the loft? Could she use them? Is she strong enough?"

"No. Definitely not."

"Lastly, Seymour, how did she get up on the wall and ceiling to tack them up? Let's go down to the barn. I want to see this for myself."

Leaving the house, Seymour and Mr. Saunders walked down the driveway, into the barn and climbed the ladder up to the loft. Melissa was asleep in her nest and looked quite peaceful. Mr. Saunders looked around, primarily at the posters, nodded his head and said he was satisfied. "It appears that she had help, Seymour, human help. Someone came up here and put these up."

"That confirms what I thought too."

Seymour and Mr. Saunders looked at each other, but nothing more was said. They climbed down from the loft and went outside into the hot summer sun. It felt good.

"What do you think, Seymour," asked Mr. Saunders. "Where did she get help like that?"

"I have no idea, but thanks for listening to me and coming to the barn, Mr. Saunders. I'll keep a close eye on her for a while and see if I can learn any more about those posters. She is one of the best mice I have ever known and I don't want to lose her. I need to get to the bottom of this."

"I understand Seymour. I'll think about this, too. In the meantime, let me know if I can be of further help."

A chill ran down his spine as Seymour watched his friend walk up to the house. He looked up at the barn. Something was seriously awry, and he wondered what could possibly have happened to his favorite niece.

Chapter 5

The House Down the Lane

Over the next two days Melissa occupied almost all of Seymour's thoughts. He watched her closely, but there was no outward sign of a problem that seemed to have any significance. She ate, played, and rested the same as the other mice. However, on the evening of the third day, after everyone had gone to bed, Melissa slowly got up from her nest and went down the ladder. Seymour was in bed as well, but awake, keeping an eye on her and he saw her leave. Where was she going at this hour, Seymour wondered. He got up and followed at a distance.

The night air was mild and the moon was still up. Mice don't need as much light as humans do to see well in the dark, so although it wasn't a full moon, it was a clear night and there was enough light for Seymour to see Melissa heading out the driveway towards the road. It was quite a long driveway, with grass fields on both sides, and about half way to the road she cut across the right hand field to Mr. Saunders's neighbor's house, Mrs. Bennett's. Seymour stayed back to ensure he was not spotted, and he saw Melissa walk up the back stairs to a screened porch. She went up onto the porch and then into the house itself. Seymour ran up to the stairs then stopped. Should he follow? What if he was caught? Would it help or hurt Melissa? On the other hand, what if she was in danger and he was not there to help? He decided to follow; he really needed to know why she was acting so strangely and why she would go to a neighbor's house, especially at night.

Mrs. Bennett's house was quite large and from the outside looked somewhat similar to Mr. Saunders's house. Seymour had never been inside though, and did not know the layout. Nor could he see the inside of the house from where he was. He knew he had to get closer and look in a window or an open door to keep tabs on Melissa, so he climbed up the stairs just as Melissa had. Keeping very quiet, he crept through the porch door that was slightly ajar and tiptoed across the porch and up to the door that led to the inside of the house. It was closed. Seymour was puzzled; he knew Melissa could not have opened that door herself, and he did not hear it open or close. He was quite sure she had not come out of the house, so where was she? And, if she got in the house, how did she do it? He waited and listened for a long time but heard nothing but a few muffled sounds. The door to the house had glass panes near the top, and with some difficulty he was able to climb up to one of them. He sat there easily enough on the window frame, but after a while, hearing or seeing nothing more inside, he climbed down the stairs and decided to wait out in the lawn among some flowers.

The moon was setting by the time Melissa finally emerged. Seymour saw that she was carrying a small package and was heading back to the barn the same way she had come, across the lawn and field, and back down the long driveway. He could see that she was not being followed, and could see no one else in the area, animals or people. He thought it best not to call out or interrupt her as she traveled, so he just stayed behind her to see that no harm befell her. Once at the barn, Melissa went right up to the loft, still carrying the package that she got at Mrs. Bennett's house. She went directly to her nest, with Seymour following unobserved. He watched as she climbed into bed and was fast asleep in just a few moments. Seymour quietly approached her and looked around but did not see the package. He knew he would find it sooner or later as there were very few places in the barn where it could be hidden. Being a patient mouse, he would wait for Melissa to wake up and then see where it was.

In the morning it was business as usual for the mice. They arose and, as was the rule, straightened up around their little beds, washed their hands and feet, and ate whatever breakfast they had gathered from the floors of the stalls or was saved from the day before. It usually consisted of crumbs, kernels of corn, pieces of apples and carrots, or feed that the horses spilled. Seymour noticed, though, that Melissa's breakfast was very different: it was cat food!

The fact that there was cat food available was not unusual, as Mr. and Mrs. Saunders did feed Seek, the barn cat, in one of the unoccupied horse stalls. But there was a hard and fast rule, and the mice all knew it, not to take food from the cat's dish; it would put a mouse in too much danger. The cat was almost always nearby, and mice would be a tasty treat. Eating the cat's food would surely antagonize the cat, which could also lead to very unpleasant consequences.

Seymour went over to Melissa as she was eating and said, "Good morning, Melissa, how are you today?"

"Fine, Seymour, how are you," said Melissa.

"Very well, thank you," replied Seymour. "What have you got there for breakfast?"

"Cat food, of course. I really like it a lot. It's very tasty, and much more nutritious than mere bits of corn or horse feed, don't you think?"

"Really, Melissa? Where did you learn that?"

"Lesson three in our program, Seymour. It's all about why cats must eat so differently from mice, or dogs, or humans. We cats need a diet of almost 100% protein. It is much more advanced nutrition, which is in keeping with cats being much more advanced animals."

"You said, 'we cats', Melissa? Hmmm. And 'lesson three', you said? Is that some sort of program that Mrs. Bear teaches?" he asked.

All the mice, as well as the other animals in the woods and meadows behind the barn and the Saunders's house, went to Mrs. Bear's school whenever they needed supplemental training that their natural environment and their parents or siblings didn't supply. But Melissa had not gone to Mrs. Bear's school for a year or more, and up to a day or so ago, she was eating exactly the same food as the other mice. So in addition to the new lessons, Seymour wondered where the cat food came from.

"What are lessons one and two, Melissa," Seymour asked.

"Let's see. Lesson one is why cats are the best animals in the world. Lesson two is how to become a cat if you are not born one. Lesson three, as I said, is how to eat like a cat. Lesson four, which we will start soon, is how to act, walk, talk and live like a cat. Lesson five is how to kill like a cat. And I forget the other lessons. But I will know them all soon. There are ten or twelve all together, I think." Melissa said, looking at Seymour with a smile and feeling proud that she was doing so well with her studies.

"Very impressive, Melissa", Seymour stammered. "Where do you take these lessons? Are there books or lectures you must attend? Is there a school?"

"No, Seymour, I just know these things. The thoughts are in my head. It is so easy to remember these facts. That's what makes it so good." Melissa stood up, ready to leave. "I'm finished with my breakfast, can I go play now?"

"Sure," said Seymour. "Run along."

Chapter 6

Seymour Finds Evidence

Seymour was now convinced that something very strange and potentially harmful for the mice was underway. What it was, he had no clue, but he made up his mind to find out. The first thing he did was check over Melissa's nest and living quarters more carefully, looking for the backpack she'd carried last night and anything else that might help him figure out what was going on. He looked at the posters for any sign of where she could have found them. Some were from magazines, he could see that, others were more likely store-bought, but he could find no tags or indication of where they were purchased. They were fastened to the inside of the barn roof, which slanted over many of the mice's nests, and secured with pushpins. Those were in good supply in the barn itself, as Mrs. Saunders often used them to stick up instructions on how to care for the horses when she and Mr. Saunders traveled, so no helpful information there either. One thing was certain: as Mr. Saunders had surmised, Melissa could not have put the posters up by herself.

Nothing looked different about her bed, in or underneath it, or among any of her other belongings. The mice did not need much in the way of clothes or furniture, so there was really nothing else to examine. Just when he was about to give up and go back below, he spied something poking out from under her pillow. It was a small tape recorder with a cord attached that lead to a set of tiny earphones. Next to it was the backpack that Melissa carried home from Mrs. Bennett's house. Seymour put the earphones on, and pushed play. What he heard shocked him to his very core.

"You are sleepy now, so close your eyes and just listen," a woman's soothing voice said, first in mouse and then English. "You know that cats are the kindest, most gentle animals in the world, and everyone wants to be one. Before this program was announced, that was impossible. Sadly, if you were not born a cat, you had to remain whatever animal you were. But now you have a great opportunity to be someone better. You are on your way to joining us. Yes, you too can actually become a cat."

Seymour had heard enough. He took the tape recorder and earphones and headed up to see Mr. Saunders again. When Mr. Saunders heard the knocking and saw who was at the door, he invited Seymour in. Once seated, he brought Mr. Saunders up to date about how he followed Melissa to Mrs. Bennett's house, where she stayed for hours, and where she had obtained a backpack with the tape recorder in it, he then followed her home. And this morning he had listened to the tape.

Seymour passed over the recorder and earphones to Mr. Saunders and said, "I believe that you need to hear this too." The earphones were designed for a mouse and so were quite small, but Saunders put one of the speakers to his ear and listened. After a few minutes he took them off. His face was deadly serious, and his complexion was ashen. He shook his head in disbelief. What he then said to Seymour was very disquieting.

"It appears that someone has singled out your Melissa for some sort of experiment, Seymour, possibly some sort of mind control or brainwashing. The question is who, and why? Why would someone other than a cat want to suggest to a mouse that they want to become a cat? It makes no sense. Mice hate and fear cats, as well they should. And here is Melissa, running around pretending she's a cat? What on earth could possibly be gained by that, Seymour?"

"I wish I knew," said Seymour. "But you said mind control or brainwashing? I've never heard those terms before, and it would help if I knew more about it. I also think that we would be closer to the answers to our questions if we knew who actually made that tape. I believe Melissa got it at Mrs. Bennett's house. Was it she who made it, or someone else? And as you point out, to what end?"

"You are right there, Seymour, those are all good questions. I think we may learn more if we consult a specialist in this area. Let's get to someone who really knows."

Chapter 7

A Visit to Rutgers University

Mr. Saunders went to the phone and called his good friend, Dr. Charles Liu, a professor in the Business School at Rutgers University. Dr. Liu answered on the second ring.

"Ted," said Dr. Liu, "it is good to hear your voice. I hope you are well. What can I do for you?"

Mr. Saunders related a brief summary of the problem. "That is quite an interesting story, Ted," said Dr. Liu. "Unfortunately, I am not an expert in this area. You need to speak with someone in the field of brainwashing and mind control, and those disciplines are in the Psychology Department."

Mr. Saunders was, of course, aware of that but he did not know who would be the best one to contact in that department. Although Dr. Liu's expertise was management, Mr. Saunders also knew that he was acquainted with many of the other disciplines and faculty at Rutgers.

Dr. Liu thought for a moment and said, "I believe we have one of the best teams in the country right here in New Jersey, under the leadership of Dr. Kenneth Langley, a noted authority on mind control. Let me see what I can tell you. I am reading here from an announcement we received a week or so ago. There's a Dr. Antonio T. DeStefano, who recently transferred to Rutgers from the University of Nevada, Martin

Goldsmith from the University of Chicago, Laszlo Somogy from the Polytechnia of Bucharest in Romania, and Peter Dempsey from Columbia University. They are here to work on a government grant that we received and will work with Dr. Langley. I heard him and DeStefano speak a few weeks ago at a symposium I attended. They are both very knowledgeable and may be able to help. Hold on a moment and I'll talk to the team's administrative secretary and see if either of them has time on their calendar to meet with you."

Mr. Saunders turned to Seymour and said, "I'm on hold here, so please help yourself to some soda or tea." Seymour told him water was fine, and hopped up on the counter next to the sink and ran some cold water into a little glass that Mrs. Saunders kept there just for him.

A few moments later Dr. Liu came back on the line and said, "Ted, DeStefano has a class at two PM today, and a staff meeting at five, so how about 3:30 or 4:00 this afternoon in his office in the Psych Building? I did tell him that it would be a strange pair coming to see him, but nothing more. I'll leave it up to you to explain about Seymour." A longtime friend of Mr. Saunders, Dr. Liu was familiar with the extraordinary mouse that lived in his barn.

"That's great, Charles", Mr. Saunders responded. "Please tell him thanks, and we'll see him at 4:00. And thank you, too."

"My pleasure, Ted," said Dr. Liu. "Please keep me posted; this is quite an intriguing story."

Seymour and Mr. Saunders agreed to meet at three o'clock for the short drive to New Brunswick. In the meantime, back at the barn Seymour went on line to find out what he could on his own about mind control. He Googled brainwashing, read up on that subject, then moved to mind control, thought control and related subjects. There was quite a lot of information available, much of it fascinating. He was absorbed in the topic, but time was getting away from him and he saw that it was almost three, so he went back up to the house and met Mr. Saunders.

Seymour told Mr. Saunders about what he had learned as they drove, and they discussed a few points, but both knew that the meeting with Dr. DeStefano was an important step. They simply did not know enough about what was going on with Melissa and hoped that DeStefano could shed some light on the problem.

Mr. Saunders parked his car in one of the large student lots on the Rutgers campus and they headed to the Psychology building. Seymour checked his watch; it was a little bit after 3:30. As they walked, they turned quite a few heads: it was unlikely anyone had ever seen a mouse strolling alongside a human before! Not only was Seymour an extraordinarily gifted mouse, he was quite distinguished looking as well. He was larger than most mice, and he held himself erect with a certain wellborn posture and bearing. He had a directness of gaze that never failed to draw attention from humans and other animals. Several people stopped the pair and inquired if this was a pet mouse, and Seymour, looking straight at the inquisitor, was quick to respond that he was in no way a pet. Once they got over the shock of a walking and talking mouse, people apologized and left the two alone. They entered the building, located the office where Dr. DeStefano worked and knocked on the door. When they heard a response to enter, they did.

Three people greeted them. In addition to Dr. DeStefano, two members of the team were there, Langley and Goldsmith. After introductions, they got the surprise of the week when they saw and heard a mouse speak. Mr. Saunders began to explain a bit about Seymour, and why they had come. Checking the time, Drs. Langley and Goldsmith excused themselves as they had other matters to attend to, and left Mr. Saunders and Seymour with Dr. DeStefano. They took the chairs offered to them and sat down as Dr. DeStefano, clearly fascinated with these visitors, asked how he could help.

Seymour provided some background on the situation, talked about the mice in the barn, Melissa's belief that she was a cat, the posters near her bed, the "lessons" she cited, and the tape-recorded message. He also noted that he had read a bit about the topic on the Web. He handed over the tape and the earphones to Dr. DeStefano, who turned on the recorder and listened intently.

"As they walked they turned quite a few heads ...

When he had finished listening, he turned back and said, "Hmmm, that is very interesting. Okay, a little background about mind control that might not have been on the Web. In layman's terms, it involves 'imprinting' into the subject's brain some ideas and thoughts to subvert his own control of his brain. It can be as benign as subliminal advertising, or as harmful as kidnapping people, keeping them in cults, and forcing them to break the law.

"Some believe that brainwashing is really just another form of hypnosis, which has been around for hundreds of years and is not at all dangerous when in the right hands. But it's not the same at all. With hypnosis you have to want to be hypnotized, and you will never do anything under hypnosis that you would not otherwise do. Further, hypnosis puts you in a pleasant, deeply relaxed state and usually causes you to feel refreshed after a session. The purpose of hypnotherapy is to help the patient overcome some issue from the past, or an addiction, or perhaps deal with a phobia. The medical professional that uses hypnotherapy seeks to make his patient a happy, productive member of the community. Brainwashing, in comparison, is done without the patient's consent. It forces the subject's body into a hypnotic state through techniques such as intimidation, starvation, narcotics, or sleep deprivation, and seeks to isolate him completely from the rest of society. In essence, the goal of brainwashing is to make the subject do something he doesn't want to do.

"Some claim that 'brainwashing', which is a crude term for it, can only be done with the subject's willing participation. But it can also employ more involved measures, such as actual medical procedures and/ or surgery, where wires and other devices are implanted in the subject's brain, altering their behavior forever. When these measures were tried in the past they were limited to one individual, with mixed results. Are you following me, gentlemen?"

"I am," said Seymour, and Mr. Saunders nodded his head. DeStefano continued. "Having an organized program to do it on a mass scale is a lot more recent, and more difficult to implement. The first we knew about it was in the 1930s, when 'brainwashing' was put into practice by countries like Germany, Russia, China and North

Korea, whose intent was to have the government control people's beliefs and behavior. There was a movie called "*The Manchurian Candidate*", where the Chinese and North Koreans brainwashed an American prisoner of war and programmed him to kill a United States presidential candidate. The CIA had a strong interest in this subject and initiated a project labeled Monarch Mind-Controlled Programming. This program was named 'Monarch' because scientists had learned that a Monarch butterfly knows intuitively where it was born (its roots) and it passes this knowledge via genetics on to its offspring, from generation to generation. This was one of the key species that tipped scientists off to the fact that knowledge can be, and is, passed genetically. This information was deadly in the hands of skillful scientific "programmers', who carried this logic to the extreme, using electroshock, torture, abuse and mind games, and forced their subjects to dissociate from reality. Their objective was to create a victim who would follow directives with no conscious awareness, including execution of acts in clear violation of the victim's moral principles, spiritual convictions, and free will. The victim in turn could pass these traits on to his children, creating generations of 'robot-like' people. We in the U.S. concluded that we would not engage in it.

"In 1957, sociologist Albert D. Biderman published a well-received article on how one can use coercion to achieve the compliance of an individual. He listed practices such as isolation, monopolization of perception, induced debility and exhaustion, occasional indulgences, and devaluing of the individual as methods of brainwashing. So these are techniques one must be on the lookout for. However, to my knowledge this has never been successful in animals, although several scientists, including some on the forefront of mind control, such as David Bromley, Anson Shupe, and Laszlo Somogyi, have tried it with squid and dolphins with no positive outcomes. And we all remember the use of brainwashing in the allegorical novel by George Orwell, *Animal Farm*. In that work, the pigs convince the other animals that they are superior, but they revert to behaving like humans, leaving their animal senses behind. But that, as we know, is fiction."

Seymour and Mr. Saunders looked at each other, absorbing the seriousness of what was being said. They were dumbfounded.

Chapter 8

Brainwashing Continued

"So, I believe there are at least two major questions here," said Seymour. "First, if someone is trying to brainwash and control Melissa's mind, and possibly doing the same to other mice, which it appears they are doing given the tape we heard, why would they do it? And next, what other methods do you think they are using to achieve their ends?"

Dr. DeStefano sat back in his chair and thought out loud. "I don't know why someone would think it could work on mice, since it has been proven that they are not the most intelligent of animals. Uh, no slight intended, Seymour. But we can come back to that point later.

"As for techniques, they would most likely use methods such as electric shock and behavior control to start. They might also consider the use of some mind-altering drugs, such as Scopolamine. Then they would progress to such things as changing someone's physical reality, using group sessions and rituals, deferring to superiors, rewards and punishment. Also a sense of individualism is discouraged and "group think" prevails. There is a strong need for obedience in the group or cult. There is usually a 'Master' who is in charge. After he or she is introduced as the only one to believe, they will employ information control. The Master's people will use quite a bit of deception and false information, but make it sound as if it is fact. Spying on others is encouraged to insure cooperation by all.

"Then when the subject is ready, thought control techniques are used. The people in charge introduce so called 'truth' words to reduce very complex ideas to simple clichés, which the subject memorizes. They will introduce ideas that the subject then alters and twists into what the Master wants the subject to understand. Here they may use electric shock again, to have the victim want to please their handlers and avoid pain. They will also manipulate memories and change the past experience into a new one that replaces the earlier memory. No criticism of the leaders is allowed; only good thoughts about their Master are permitted. They usually use hypnotism to accomplish this.

"Lastly, they will use emotion control, such as saying that if there are any problems they can always come to the Master for support. And if there are mistakes, it is always the subject's doing, never the Master's. They will use fear as a normal threat: fear of being shut out from the group or cult, fear of the Master, since the subject at this point cannot see or visualize the future except as part of the group. If it works, when finished the subject has become a different person ~ or in this case, mouse. They have a new identity."

Seymour and Mr. Saunders looked at one another in alarm. "Doctor," Seymour said gravely, "You have described what I am already seeing in Melissa. She thinks she is a cat. There are 'lessons' and, as you heard, tapes using thought control to convince her of that. If these are the early steps, what can we do?"

"My advice is to find out where this group or cult is meeting and observe their process," said Dr. DeStefano. "Determine what specific methods they are employing, see how many mice are involved, that sort of thing. Next, find out, if you can, who the Master is, the real expert behind this, and what his or her objective might be. I doubt the person living next to you, whom you have described as a fairly normal neighbor, is the true Master. She is most likely a level or two down in the hierarchy. It has to be someone else, a scientist, someone who is very skilled at these techniques. Learning the identity of the Master will undoubtedly give us a clue as to why they are experimenting with mice and what they are trying to achieve.

"As for your Melissa, I hope we can free her from this group and save her. It will take some time and a lot of work, but many have had success when they employ a mix of deprogramming interventions and exit counseling techniques. I have written several papers on these steps and will provide you with copies. These interventions are the latest protocols we have. If you follow them, they should work. I only say 'should' because we have not used them on animals, only humans. But from what you tell me, you need to act quickly. Every day you delay, your friend Melissa is drawn further into their control."

Dr. DeStefano looked at his watch. "I apologize, but I must cut this meeting short," he said. "I have a television interview in a little while and must prepare for it, so this is all the time I have today. Please call me, though, if you need additional help. This is a fascinating case, and I will be interested in hearing more about it, and helping as much as I can."

He reached into his desk and pulled some papers from his files. They were the deprogramming papers. He attached his business card to them and passed them to Seymour.

"Good luck, Seymour."

"Thank you, Doctor," said Seymour as they shook hands. "It appears to me that we are going to need it."

Chapter 9

Seymour Follows Melissa Again

It was a quiet ride home. Both Seymour and Mr. Saunders were lost in their own thoughts. Seymour had already made up his mind about what he needed to do.

Back in the barn he returned the tape recorder to Melissa's nest, lest she become suspicious. Then he read the information on deprogramming he received from Dr. DeStefano and concluded it would take time to get Melissa back to where she was before – if it was possible at all. It did not look good for her, but Seymour was determined to do whatever it took to save her.

When everyone was asleep, Melissa, as before, got up and went down the ladder and out the barn door. Seymour was ready and followed her to Mrs. Bennett's house. This time, however, he saw that the door was propped open and after Melissa entered he counted to five and then slipped in. All the lights in the house were on and it was very quiet. Spooky quiet, Seymour thought. Because Melissa was under a spell and thought she was a cat, he knew there could be real cats here, and he did not want to encounter any. So once inside, he stayed behind her and tracked Melissa through several rooms. He remained as low and guarded as he could, and kept a sharp eye out for any animals or humans. He saw her walk through another open door and down a flight of stairs.

"My name, as you know, is Tiger Tail ..."

Seymour now moved even more slowly and carefully. Finally, certain that he was not being watched, he too went through the door and down the stairs, but not all the way to the bottom. From his position halfway down the stairs and still well hidden, he could see Melissa in a hallway. She hesitated a moment, looked around, and then went through another open door and into a large room. Seymour followed quietly down the last few steps. He figured that they were now in the basement of the house. Staying in the shadows, he ran along a wall and into the room that Melissa had entered. He hid under a chair.

The shades in the room were drawn, and the lights were on a low setting. A projector screen was set up facing two rows of benches upon which sat about ten mice. The only one Seymour recognized was Melissa. There was silence in the room, and the mice sat facing the screen, which was blank. They all sat without moving. That in itself was alarming to Seymour, because he knew only too well how very hard it is for mice to sit still for any length of time. Then the lights were turned off and the screen came to life.

On the screen was a large marmalade cat, speaking "mouse speak" in a woman's voice. It was a pleasant, reassuring voice, and Seymour recognized it as that same voice he'd heard on the tape that he had found under Melissa's pillow.

"Thank you for coming," the cat purred. "You are well on your way to joining us cats. My name, as you know, is Tiger Tail, and tigers are the most special of all cats, colorful, fast, smart, and fierce. If you do well in our program, you too can be as fast, smart and fierce as I am. But first, there are some things I want you to do. Let's begin by learning to clean ourselves. Do as I do."

Tiger Tail lifted her paw, licked it, and stroked her face with her paw. "You see," she said. "It is important to be clean, and it is a very cat-like process. Give it a try." The mice began imitating Tiger Tail, and licked and stroked themselves just as she did. This went on for a while. Then she reminded them that they all had to do this several times a day, and if they did not, they would be punished, and perhaps not let into the group again. They could never be a cat without learning to clean themselves, and that is why they licked. They had to do it just as she did. The video went on for another twenty or so minutes, showing the mice other cat behaviors such as how to meow, how to walk like a cat, and how to hunt like a cat, stealthily and pretending not to see anything, but yet watching all around them, ready to pounce in a moment time. This was today's lesson, she said, but there were many more steps to take before they could attain true cat status.

Tiger Tail instructed them that when they went to sleep at night they must listen to their tape recorder over and over again to successfully learn these lessons. She said she would see them all here again tomorrow evening, and wished them well. "I love each and every one of you," she said. "I am counting on you to do the right thing. If you do, you will be part of Tiger Tail's group and we will be happy cats all the time." The lesson ended with Tiger Tail asking them to spread the word to other mice about being a cat, and bring them to the meetings. "Now let's stand and pledge our unity." They stood on their benches and repeated the Cat Pledge in unison, three times: "Cats are good; cats are the best; cats never eat mice." And with that the lights came up and the mice started for the door.

As soon as Seymour saw that the meeting was ending, he dashed up the stairs ahead of them. Quietly, he let himself out the door and got in a position outside the house where he could see them disperse just as he had waited for and watched Melissa before. Several mice went to Mrs. Bennett's small barn, others went into another field down the road, and Melissa headed for the home barn alone. He let her go ahead and watched her climb up the ladder into the hayloft. He followed a few minutes later, reassured that Melissa was safe and in her nest. He knew she would be listening to her lessons.

Chapter 10

Seymour Meets Mrs. Bennett

On the way home, Seymour realized that the mind control had gone on long enough, and that he had to intervene or he might never be able to save his niece. But how? Should he try to bring Melissa back to reality himself, or would that do more harm than good? Or perhaps bring Melissa to a veterinarian or to an animal mind control specialist, if there even was such a one? Then, remembering Dr. DeStefano's advice, he realized the first thing he needed to do was find the Master. Although it most likely wasn't Mrs. Bennett, it was a place to start.

The next morning, Seymour went to Mrs. Bennett's house, marched up the front steps and knocked on the door. When no one answered, he knocked again, louder. The door finally swung open.

"Yes, who is there?" Mrs. Bennett called, looking out across the narrow porch. "Who knocked," she asked, seeing no one. "Is this a joke of some kind? I know I heard a knock," she muttered to herself. Then, about to close the door, she glanced down and saw a mouse. Her face lit up in a big smile. "Oh good, a mouse!" she cried. "Would you like to come in and have a cookie? I have some special cookies I keep just for mice. I love mice," she purred, "although I do like cats better. I wish all animals could be cats, don't you? Oh, you are such a big, handsome fellow," she exclaimed.

"Would you like to come in and have a cookie?"

Seymour stood up tall and responded in English, "My name is Seymour, and I live next door in Mr. Saunders's barn."

"Eeeeeek!" screamed Mrs. Bennett, stumbling backward and then jumping on a chair in the foyer, "he's talking!" In a reasonable, soothing voice, Seymour explained to an astonished Mrs. Bennett that he was indeed able to communicate with humans, as well as with mice.

As Seymour waited for the woman to take in this phenomenon, he felt some of the pieces of the puzzle falling into place. The voice of Tiger Tail on the tape was definitely Mrs. Bennett's, and she was obviously part of the leadership of the cult trying to brainwash the mice. But how could she also speak mouse? Although he wanted to challenge her right then and there to try and make her explain herself about the mice meetings and lessons, he needed to know more and decided that showing interest in her might be the better way to reach his objective. But first, as a test, he repeated his name and where he lived in mouse speak, and Mrs. Bennett did not appear to hear him. Extraordinary, thought Seymour.

Going back to human speak, he said in a graceful, sociable way, "It's Mrs. Bennett, I believe? I have heard Mr. Saunders mention the nice lady next door, and yes, I would love some cookies, thank you." Looking around, Seymour added, "What a lovely home you have." Mrs. Bennett got down from the chair, invited him in, and they walked together to the kitchen. He saw cat pictures on all the walls, a scratching post in every room, litter boxes here and there, and small bowls of milk in the corners.

Once in the kitchen, Mrs. Bennett sat on the floor, asking Seymour to join her. She gave him two cookies, taking two for herself, and said, "Seymour, I gave you the ginger cookies because I know mice love the taste of ginger. I'll have the tuna chip." Seymour let Mrs. Bennett take a bite of her cookie before he considered whether or not to taste his. She sat there with a smile on her face, dreaming it seemed, not really watching him closely. He wondered why he and she had different cookies? He didn't particularly like ginger and to the best of his knowledge, the other mice didn't either, so where did she get the idea that they did? He pretended to eat his cookie, carefully putting several pieces into his jacket pocket when she was not looking, and he changed the subject from cookies to cats.

"You have so many cat items here, Mrs. Bennett," he said, "but I don't see any cats."

"Why those pictures are *mine,* and I am a cat, you see, so there is indeed a cat here. Me! I became one after the Master said I had progressed enough. Would you like to be a cat? I can help you. The lessons are all on tape, I recorded them myself after hearing the ones the Master had done. Mine, I have to say, are much better. The mice really enjoy them. Living in Mr. Saunders barn, you must know one of the mice in our program. She is a delightful little creature with a lovely brown coat, snowy chest and a tiny pink nose. But she will be better off when she is a cat."

Seymour was quite taken aback by this peculiar woman. "I'm not as convinced of that as you are, Mrs. Bennett. I always thought she was fine as a mouse, but I'm sure you think otherwise. And may I ask who your Master is?"

"Oh, Master is great," she gushed. "He is fine and beautiful, the most thoughtful and wonderful person, and I am so in awe of him. He is right in everything he does. He loves all animals, but he loves cats the best, and when he asked if I would like to know more about them I said I would. I do like cats, but I never had one. I have some sheep and goats in my barn, and I had two dogs, but I had to get rid of them. It would never do for them to interfere with my mice lessons, or with me since I am now a cat. The Master has a program that can change almost any animal and teach them act like another. He said I was special, and he needed my help with his work because there was too much for one person to do. I just had to say yes. He put me through his program to show me how it's done. Now, as you can see, I am truly a cat in every way.

"And I'll tell you a secret," she chattered on. "My human name is Mrs. Bennett, yes, but my real name, my cat name, is Elvira. Isn't that just a lovely name? I do believe there was someone famous who had that name and also called herself the "Princess of the Dark". Isn't that appropriate? Cats do so very well in the dark. Elvira is a much better name, don't you think? Although for the mice, I use the name Tiger Tail. By the way, Seymour, my job is to change others into cats. The Master said to start with mice; they are such docile and simple animals. So I now run this program for the mice that live nearby. We would love for you to join us, Seymour. In fact, we will be meeting here tonight."

Throughout his various adventures, helping presidents, celebrities, and other people in general need of his services, Seymour had seen a lot of unusual things for a mouse, and he hadn't thought there was much that could shock him anymore. Then he noticed that Mrs. Bennett, AKA Elvira, was now licking her hands and arms and grooming herself just like a cat. Her fingernails were filed to a point and looked surprisingly like claws. This lady was crackers!

"That is a nice offer, Mrs. Bennett," he said. "Or should I say, Elvira. Let me think it over and I'll let you know."

Seymour headed for the door, but he kept one eye on Mrs. Bennett. He really did not want to turn his back on her; he didn't trust her now. When he turned to say goodbye, he happened to look at a pile of mail on the floor. It was next to the front door, and it appeared that whoever brought it into the house just dropped it there. Some of it obviously hadn't been touched for days or even weeks, and he noticed there were letters from Verizon, American Express, local merchants, and some junk mail. But what caught his attention were several pieces from a Dr. Peter Dempsey, at the East Coast Laboratory. Seymour knew he had heard that name before, but he wasn't sure exactly where. Before he could react further, Mrs. Bennett opened the door for him. "Bye for now, Seymour," she said with a gleam in her eye. "Please stay well, and eat up. You could use a bit more weight. I do hope to see you at our session tonight," she said as she closed the door.

Chapter 11

Seymour Goes to New York

When Seymour got to his office, he took out Dr. DeStefano's card and dialed his number. The secretary put him right through. "Doctor," said Seymour, "I just came from the house where the cult group is meeting. The owner of the house is clearly under some sort of spell, as is Melissa, and when I was leaving I saw some letters from a Peter Dempsey. That name sounded familiar to me. Is he one of the scientists you mentioned who are on the cutting edge of mind control and brain-washing techniques and is now at Rutgers?"

"Yes he is, Seymour," said the doctor. "Dempsey, like the others we have here working with Langley, is one of the leading scientists in that field, one of the best, and he has also conducted his own research. He is a very competent man, and is currently travelling in Europe."

"The name on the letterhead said East Coast Laboratory," said Seymour. "Do you know anything about it?"

"East Coast Laboratory is in New York City, in the vicinity of Columbia University," replied Dr. DeStefano. "I think East Coast Labs shares some facilities and at times receives joint funding for research grants with Columbia. I believe that Dr. Dempsey is one of the founders of the lab. And as far as I know, Rutgers is not involved in any way."

"… he crossed the George Washington Bridge …"

"Can you think of any reason why he would be writing to a woman here in New Jersey," asked Seymour. "An extremely odd woman who believes she is a cat?"

"No, Seymour, but I can imagine what you're thinking."

"Thank you, Doctor, for your help. I'll be back in touch if I have any further questions."

"Seymour, be careful," cautioned Dr. DeStefano. "If Dempsey is involved with this issue, and is caught up in anything that is remotely illegal, you can bet he will not want to be exposed. I've just learned that the type of work at the level you described has been under suspicion for a while, and the Feds and the ASPCA want it outlawed here in the U.S."

Seymour went up to Mr. Saunders's house and told him what he had learned, and that he was heading into New York City to see what he could find at the offices of East Coast Laboratory. Mr. Saunders asked if Seymour wanted him to accompany him on the trip, but Seymour said no, that he had been to New York many times and he was much more likely to remain undetected if he was alone. No one paid much attention to a mouse. Mr. Saunders urged him to be careful and reminded him of Dr. DeStefano's warning that these cults may well be operating on the fringe of the law, if not outside it. Seymour assured Mr. Saunders that he would follow that advice, but he knew in his heart that caution does not always rule out aggressive action when wrongdoings are involved.

Seymour got on his computer again and Googled East Coast Labs for any new information but all he could find was an address and phone number. Knowing he would have to go there shortly, he asked Leroy, one of his most trustworthy mice, to watch over the others for a while, especially Melissa, who was behaving a bit strangely lately. Leroy assured Seymour he would look after all the mice in Seymour's absence.

Sitting back in his chair, Seymour thought for a few moments of what he might encounter when he got to the lab, and he made a list of a few items that he might need for the trip: tools, rope, his small Swiss army knife, and one or two other pieces of equipment. Before he left the loft he said goodbye to the mice and asked them to be good for Leroy.

On the ground, he packed his supplies into his school bus, his every-day vehicle specially outfitted for his slight stature, and drove off for New York City. When he crossed the George Washington Bridge from New Jersey, it was past 8:00 PM and lightly raining. As always, the traffic in the city was heavy, but he found his way down the Henry Hudson Parkway, got off at 125th Street, turned right onto Broadway and headed downtown. Using Google Maps, he located the East Coast Laboratory building on West 113th Street, between Amsterdam Avenue and Broadway, and drove slowly past it, looking at the surroundings. It was an attractive four-story brownstone building, very solid looking, and there was a sign on the door that he could not quite read. The other buildings on the block appeared to be similar in size, architecture, and age to the lab, so Seymour surmised they were all affiliated with or owned by Columbia University. The other buildings also displayed signs listing the offices inside and, although he could not quite read every word on them, they appeared to house graduate departments, academic societies and professional libraries.

113th Street was a narrow, one-way street heading west. Finding a parking space in New York City is always difficult, and Seymour had to hunt for one, finally finding a legal spot a block away, further east, just beyond Amsterdam Avenue. After parking his diminutive bus, he took a few minutes to think through the items he'd brought with him and decide which he might need. He selected a few tools, hooks, a saw and other items, and put those and the key to his bus into his sack. He left his iPhone in the glove box: he needed neither its extra weight nor bulk, and it could be disastrous if the information that was contained on it fell into the wrong hands.

Seymour knew he had to get inside unobserved if he was going to find out what was going on in that laboratory. Would anyone be there after office hours? Before he left his bus, he made a call to the lab. He got a recorded message saying that no one was there to answer the call, please leave your name and number, along with a brief message, and someone would return the call as soon as possible. The fact that no one answered was fine, but he knew there could still be people busy at work in there and just not answering the telephone, so he needed to be cautious.

Seymour approached the building very carefully, pressing closely to the walls, and he was happy to see the rain was keeping people off the street. Those who were out were huddled in their parkas or under an umbrella. He was grateful, too, that the street lamps shed very little light in the gloomy weather.

Reaching the building he looked up and saw that the sign on the door identified it as the Intercultural Resource Center and gave the hours of 9:00 AM to 6:00 PM. But if this was Dempsey's East Coast Labs, he sensed the building contained more than just the offices of an Intercultural Center. He knew that this was the address he Googled and telephoned, so he was sure that this was the building he was looking for.

Not wanting to be seen, Seymour waited for a time behind one of the few trees on the street, and when no one was passing by, he ran up the stone steps to the big front door. He jumped up and tried the handle, but it was locked. Not to be discouraged, he backed up a bit and saw an open window on the third floor. He figured that he could dig his paws and toes into the spaces between the blocks of granite and sandstone that made up the face of the building. After checking that there were no people nearby, he easily climbed up the façade of the building without using any of the fishing line or hooks that he carried in his sack. In no time at all he was sitting on the sill of the third floor window and peering in.

Although the lighting inside was dim, Seymour saw that he was looking into a normal sized room, and the window where he sat was placed midway in the street side wall. On all four sides of the room and on counters in the middle, he saw cages with animals in them. The ones he saw and smelled first were raccoons as they were right in front of him. In the small space between the raccoon cages and other cages on the counter they were facing was a walkway. In this walkway, on a wheeled cart in front of the raccoon's cage was a video player, and Seymour could hear someone saying, first in a language he did not know, then in English, "You could be a badger if you wanted to. What better

"He had dropped his guard for just a moment ..."

animal to be than a badger? Badgers are brave and fierce. They are bold hunters, admired by all." It was a large badger who appeared to be talking on the video, but it was a man's voice.

Seymour jumped down from the windowsill, landing on top of one of the raccoon cages. The animal inside snarled viciously when it heard and felt him land, and then saw him. Not stopping to see or check anything else at the moment, Seymour quickly jumped off again and ran to an open door. He was looking down a corridor that had six or seven doors leading off it. Going to the first door he came to, he climbed up the doorframe to the handle and was able to open it. Here, too, he saw cages with animals, this time snakes, and there was a video playing in this room as well, touting the merits of becoming a mongoose, telling the snakes that mongooses were best because they could beat any snake in a fight. Again, the animal in the video had a human voice speaking in what Seymour gathered was snake language as well as English.

The next room contained dogs, with a video telling them they could be a bear, that bears were one of the greatest animals in the world. Bears could be cuddly or ferocious. No animal was better than a bear.

He looked into the rooms behind all the other doors, and they all had similar set ups: animals in cages ~ foxes, coyotes, lynx and others ~ with videos telling them they could be some other animal, that they could be better than they were now by becoming their natural enemy.

Seymour thought this clearly had gone too far. He had seen what was going on with Melissa and the mice, and now here in the East Coast Laboratory his suspicions were confirmed. What scientist with an ounce of integrity would capture animals, take them out of their habitual environment, lock them in a cage against their will, and subject them to these experiments? Seymour was now convinced he knew who was behind this: Dempsey, the owner of the lab. However, he felt a more important obligation, and that was to free the animals. But what should he and what could he do at the present time? Open the cages and free them? He knew he could do that, let them loose, but there would be quite a commotion, with animals pitted against other animals here in the lab, fighting with each other, with a serious loss of life. And even if

Seymour helped them by freeing them, he could not communicate with them, and therefore could not control them. If some were able to get out of the building, where would they go in New York City? Out into the streets, in a place they knew nothing about, in a strange environment, away from their natural habitat? Some of them were dangerous animals. What if they harmed someone? No, that would not do. And he certainly could not pick them up and transport them back to the farm with him. But he had to act before the staff became alerted. Seymour needed a plan to help, and fast.

As he stood in the corridor pondering the situation trying to decide what action to take, disaster struck. He felt a net drop on him and before he knew it, he was scooped up in the air and carried into another room. Seymour had no time to react, and he let out a squeal, barely keeping his wits about him enough to keep from speaking or shouting in English. As his captor thrust him into a cage, Seymour heard him say, "So, mouse, you thought you could escape, did you? Well, I don't know how you got out, but you are back in your little cage now. Stay there!" The door slammed shut behind him.

Seymour couldn't believe it. He had dropped his guard for just a moment, lost his focus, and now, he himself was caught!

Chapter 12

Caged!

Seymour used slow breathing to steady himself and regain his composure. Looking around, he saw that he was surrounded on both sides by mice in cages, with rats on the other side of the room. Amazingly, he still had his small sack with the tools in it; the man who caught him never saw it. Seymour felt that he could get at the lock or pry his way out as long as they didn't find it and take it away. With all of his past adventures, he was no stranger to being in trouble; it was not all that daunting to him, as long as he could free himself when he needed to.

The wire mesh cage was small, only about two feet long by a foot wide and less than a foot high, with shavings on the floor, furnished with a water bowl and a food dish. There was not really any good place to hide his sack. When he heard the man, presumably an attendant, returning, he pushed the sack into a corner and covered it with shavings; that was the best he could do given the circumstances. The attendant set up a video player in front of his cage and pushed play. It was the same man's voice as was on the videos for the other animals, now in both mouse language and English, and the message was essentially the same as the one that Mrs. Bennett gave to Melissa and the others in her house, telling them how wonderful cats were, and ending in the pledge, "Cats are good; cats are the best; cats never eat mice."

Once the attendant was satisfied that the video was playing properly, he left. It was on a loop and continued to replay the message, over and over, and Seymour tried to block it out of his head. He could see into the cage of the mouse on his left side. That mouse was watching the video, transfixed, and Seymour could see him mouth the pledge each time it was played. In the dim light, Seymour could see that the mouse had tears in his eyes as he recited the pledge; apparently the message was hitting home. The same was true with the mouse to the right. He, too, was mesmerized, but he appeared a bit more frightened and less sympathetic. Seymour was stunned: the mind control was working to some degree, even though the mice were not willing subjects. He could tell they did not want to be there, that they were participating against their will, but still listening to the voice. He could not tell about the raccoons, the dogs, or the snakes next door, as they were not as close to him, but it definitely seemed to be working on the mice.

He knew he had to stop this "science gone mad" operation and bust it wide open by calling the authorities, but he was locked in a cage. Using the time to think about a plan, he had a number of questions. Who was in charge here? Who was "The Master", Dempsey? And if Dr. Dempsey was behind all this, as Seymour thought he might be, were some of the others like Langley, Goldsmith, Somogyi, and even DeStefano involved? Was it Dempsey who created the videos, or someone else? What technologies were involved to make them able to communicate in both native animal language and English, and who was supplying the money behind this operation? Where did Mrs. Bennett fit in, and how was she able to make her version of the recording? In the back of his mind was a very dark question: why did the scientists utilize both "animal speak" and English? Was it possible this entire project was a stepping-stone to having the program work on humans?

Clearly, Seymour had more questions than answers. Although he knew he needed to focus on how he was going to get out of there and contact someone who could help, he felt he had to know more and get to the bottom of it, and stop it. He had to expose the people at the top of this organization, whether it was just the East Coast Laboratories, or

Columbia University, or both. However, what was the best way? Should he stay in the cage for a while? Would he learn more if he remained a prisoner than if he got out and called for help? He had to decide. For a moment he regretted leaving his iPhone in the bus; he could have contacted Mr. Saunders, or called 911. But even if he had brought his cell phone, he realized he would never have been able to hide it. The attendant would have found it and his sack, and would have wondered why a mouse had such items.

Seymour paced back and forth, mentally blocking out the repetition that came from the video recording while he decided what to do. Seeing the trapped mice and other animals being kept prisoners, it didn't take long for him to make up his mind. He needed to learn more about the lab, starting with identifying the mastermind behind the program. The best way to do that was to stay here and see if anyone else besides the attendants showed up.

But he had to get out of the cage now and do some exploring. He still had his sack with his tools, and knew that if they found it, he would have no way to escape; he would be stuck there, a prisoner just as the other animals were, at least until help came. And if he did not get out, but waited for outside help, Mr. Saunders would surely figure out where he was. But that could take days, and spending that much time in the lab was not something Seymour wanted to think about. Better to act now while he had the chance.

It was late in the evening and, as far as he knew, there was only the one attendant on duty. He had the benefit of the sound of the videos playing to hide any small noises he made, and there was little light in the room other than the glow from the video monitor, so he presumed he would be difficult to see. And of course moving about in the scant light was not a problem for a mouse.

He opened his sack and took out his small Swiss army knife. Selecting the saw blade, he cut though one wire at the bottom of the cage near the back, leaving it in place and still connected on the top at the cross piece so that it would appear secure to anyone looking in. He noted that none of the other mice were paying any attention to him, and he saw that the attendant was near the door to the corridor, reading a magazine by the corridor's ceiling light. Seymour thought that his normal evening routine probably included reading and possibly dozing off for a while. Good. He cut through the next wire and, surveying his work, decided that there was just enough room for him to wiggle out if he bent these two wires a bit. To be more certain that his cuts in the wire were not detected, he had to hide them somewhat better. They were in the back of the cage, and even though he figured they were pretty difficult to see, he pushed some of the shavings up against them to be sure. Then he put the knife back in the sack and stowed it away again. This whole procedure couldn't have taken more than 15 minutes.

Seymour knew he should wait for another hour or so to better learn the attendant's routine, to see whether he made regular rounds and so might discover that the mouse that he had just found was missing from his cage. But Seymour was not content to sit and wait. He figured he could get out of his cage and back in again as long as he was careful. He needed to find out as much as he could about this laboratory, and he might not get another chance. So he slipped out of the opening, crawled down the front of the counter, and quietly went to the corridor where the attendant sat. Indeed, he was napping, making a slight snoring sound.

Seymour moved slowly past him, watching for any movement. In the corridor, he saw doors on the other side from where the animals were, and he went in the first one that was open. It appeared to be a storage room for animal feed, office and cleaning supplies, some tools and a rack of white lab coats. Nothing there of interest, he thought. He exited and crept to the next door, labeled Dr. Dempsey. It was also open, and he went in. Although it was dark, he could see it was an office furnished with a desk and one file cabinet. That was promising. That's what he wanted, some written material that might explain the purpose of the Lab, its history, and the names of those involved. He jumped up on the desk to see if there were records or correspondence he could read. The desk itself was cleared off, but how about the drawers? Strangely, there were no handles on them. It would be very difficult for Seymour to open the drawers without something to pry them open and almost impossible if the desk drawers were locked. He didn't dare go back to pick up his sack from the cage where he had some hooks, and pass the attendant again so he crept back to the supply room, where he found a dustpan. Carrying it back to the office balanced on his head so that it made no noise, he got on the chair in front of the desk and positioned himself where he could insert the pan and lever the top drawer to open it. He did this very carefully and quietly, and it worked! The desk was not locked and the drawer slid open.

There were indeed files, quite a few of them in hanging folders. The dim glow coming in the window from the streetlights in the "city that never sleeps" would not have been enough to enable human eyes to read, but it was not a problem for a mouse. Seymour saw that the files were organized by animal species, in alphabetical order. He read through one but saw no names, just dates and medical records of animals that were being tested. Working quietly through the remaining drawers, he found more of the same: animal statistics. Disappointed but not seriously concerned, he turned his attention to the file cabinet.

Seymour placed the dustpan on the floor and jumped from the desk to the top of the cabinet. He could see immediately that the dustpan would not work here because the cabinets were designed to be opened by a human hand, using a thumb and sliding the locking mechanism to the right. How could a mouse do that? Seymour had an idea. Back in the storage room he found a roll of string and some duct tape, which he carried to the office. Again, very quietly, he wrapped the string around the thumb release, secured it with duct tape, got on the opposite side of the cabinet and pulled. Presto! The top drawer snapped open just enough for him to see the content. More folders, containing what he thought were hundreds of pages of notes, many written by hand, others typed. This would take some time, so Seymour got right to work. He stopped frequently to listen for the attendant's footsteps and after a while, hearing none, he ran to the door and looked down the corridor. The man was still asleep. Seymour got back up on the file cabinet and continued to read, but he knew he had to keep track of time, and frequently checked the windows. He had to get back into the cage before the lab opened in the morning.

Most of the papers had to do with the laws on animal care, but one folder caught his interest. Labeled "Veterinary Care", it clearly proved not to be about care for the animals. It was about torture and brainwashing! Apparently, using these techniques on animals had been going on at the lab for some time under a blanket of secrecy. Unfortunately, there was no mention of a Dr. Dempsey or of any other senior medical or veterinary doctor, only a "person one" and "person two".

After spending hours in the office, going through four of the five drawers in the file cabinet, Seymour was getting concerned that all the reading he did would lead to nothing about the underlying purpose of the lab beyond what he already knew. Yes, he had found concrete evidence of wrongdoing, here in the notes and in the lab itself that was for sure, brainwashing, and articles referring to changing an animal's natural state into another state, often the animal's opposite. But in the desk and file cabinet up to this point there was nothing tying Dr. Dempsey or this lab to any crimes beyond these.

Opening the bottom drawer, he found only one item, a sealed manila envelope on the front of which was written, "The Attila Dome". Could it be what he was looking for, or just another false lead? This was his last hope as it was beginning to get light outside and he had been through all the files in this office. He opened the envelope as delicately as he could, careful to avoid ripping it or making any noise.

There was only one piece of paper inside. The typing began with a paragraph that referenced the earlier work of Dr. Somogyi when he was in Romania experimenting in the field of mind control, especially with animals. It noted what the successes and failures had been and stated that this work was halted too soon and needed to be restarted on a grand scale to create a group of willing subjects who would do the bidding of the Master. It outlined a four-stage process to achieve these goals: "Stage 1- With the animals, change them to the opposite. Stage 2 - When they are stabilized, create the trigger. Stage 3 - Expand the work to humans. Stage 4 - Initiate Attila Dome in America, Europe and

Asia. To these goals, we pledge our work and our lives." It was signed and dated last month by Enrico Gonzalez and Dr. Peter Dempsey!

Seymour knew what a dome was, and he also had a vague recollection of who Attila was, known today as Attila the Hun, a fierce warrior who sought to capture and control most of Eastern Europe and parts of Asia in the 5th century. However it was the four-stage process that brought him fully awake. Here was the first piece of the proof he needed regarding why Melissa and these other animals were captured and brainwashed. Although the evidence was scanty, he could see that changing the basic nature of animals was only the first step in a much wider and more sinister scheme to create and put into place a group of humans who would be programed to do what a "Master" told them, even though it was against their nature. He put the envelope back, closed the file drawer and went back to the door. The attendant's head was on his chest and he was fast asleep. Seymour quietly went back to his cage, his mind in turmoil.

Chapter 13

The Doctor Is In

With the video running it was hard to sleep, but Seymour did manage to get some rest. In the morning the lights suddenly came on and he saw a different attendant, not the one who captured him, push a cart carrying food and water into the room. He wore a white lab coat and went from cage to cage, filling the animals' dishes and turning off the videos as he went. Seymour was grateful for the quiet. The attendant talked to each animal as he went, and Seymour reminded himself that he could not answer if spoken to. He practiced putting a blank stare on his face and, as the attendant neared his cage, he lay down.

"So, how are we this morning, Mr. Cat," said the attendant, not really waiting for a response as he opened the door and reached in for Seymour's food dish. Seymour saw he had a nametag and that his name was Ricky. "You should like this Seafood Platter I'm giving you. Cats love it. Are you learning from the video? I hope so. Here's some water too. See you later," he said as he closed the door and moved to the next cage. Seymour noticed that he had a Spanish accent, which was fairly commonplace in New York City.

As the attendant went from cage to cage, droning the same listless greeting to each animal, Seymour stayed very still, watching until the man left the room. He noticed that there was no noise except for the sound of mice and other animals eating. No squeaking, no barking, growling, or purring; nothing. Interesting, Seymour thought. The natural animal behaviors were being altered.

The morning turned into afternoon, and now the videos were on again. Time passed slowly, and Seymour grew very tired of hearing a voice on the video explain over and over again how good cats were, and why he should long to become one. He recalled the early stages of brainwashing that Dr. Biderman wrote about some years before: isolation and monopolization of perception. Despite his efforts to ignore the voice, Seymour realized that those were feelings that he was beginning to experience.

He decided he should leave while he had the chance, call the authorities, and get the lab shut down. But then he stopped himself. Seymour realized he really could not yet directly prove anything about the purpose of the lab, other than that it might be Stage One to Attila Dome. But what if it wasn't? Perhaps the work here at the lab had nothing to do with the Attila Dome project if in fact that project really existed. He told himself that unfortunately the note by itself in the manila envelope proved almost nothing by itself. Seymour had no details about the four steps of Attila Dome. There were no specifics of why or where this plan which appeared to Seymour as sinister might happen, or when, and who else might be involved. It could refer to a book they were writing, or even a movie they hoped to produce.

He had to admit that although he and Mr. Saunders were shocked with the changes to Melissa, which including the tapes she listened to, and the video of Tiger Tail talking to mice in Mrs. Bennett's house he himself had seen nothing that would be considered brutal torture. And here in the New York lab, the only brainwashing he witnessed was animals listening to the videos. So, at the end of the day the tactics Seymour saw used on Melissa and these animals were mild. These scientists, with their PhD's and international reputations, could argue that testing animals in a university was in fact a routine matter. Also, although Columbia University had no College of Veterinary Medicine, they did have labs in the Psychology and Medical Departments, and laboratories are needed in these disciplines. And Seymour had not seen yet who was in charge here. So he was on the fence about leaving without more proof.

Then the door opened and the attendant Ricky returned, accompanied by another man in a white lab coat. They proceeded from cage to cage, examining the animals, making notes on a clipboard as they went. As they came closer Seymour could hear them more clearly and distinguish the voices. He knew Ricky's voice from this morning when he was fed, and he suddenly recognized the other as the voice from the videos. Could this be the Dr. Dempsey that he was so interested in? If it was, Seymour would have absolute proof that he was at least one of the people in charge here.

They arrived at Seymour's cage and he could see a nametag. Wait. The name was not Dempsey, it was Somogyi. Dr. Laszlo Somogyi! Seymour could now tie Dr. Somogyi directly to the lab. But where was Dempsey? There was just Somogyi and a lab attendant here. It would be a lot better if he could find Dempsey as well, right here where the animals were being kept against their will and brainwashed. Then he could also tie Dempsey to the lab and the Attila Dome initiative. Seymour crouched down and put on his blank stare again.

Dr. Somogyi took a good look into the cage. This mouse was bigger than the others, the doctor saw, with a very handsome conformation and coat, but he did not remember seeing him before. That was strange: he was such a fine specimen, surely he would have stood out. Exactly where did he come from?

Now Dr. Somogyi was intrigued. He was quite sure that this was not one of the mice that they had originally captured and entered into his program. He turned to his assistant.

"Ricky, what is this mouse doing in this cage?" he demanded.

"Which mouse, Doctor?"

"Why, this one, you fool, right in front of you, here in cage 23," barked the doctor.

"I don't know, Doctor. It was here when I did my rounds this morning, so I fed it."

Dr. Somogyi referred to his notes. "Yesterday this cage was empty. Did someone put another mouse in here? Is this a new mouse? Who was on duty last night?"

"I took over from Evans earlier this morning, Doctor, so I assume he was on all night."

"Call him, now. Wake him up if necessary and ask him where this mouse came from. If he belongs in another cage, put him back in the correct cage. If he is new, we cannot have a laboratory animal that was not properly examined and vetted. I will not permit it. It could alter the test results. Go. I will stay here."

The attendant quickly left the room to make the telephone call while Dr. Somogyi moved closer and peered into the cage, looking directly at Seymour's eyes. What was he looking for, Seymour wondered?

"We will determine whether you have been here for a while, or if you are a new mouse that my stupid assistant picked up and placed here," said Dr. Somogyi. "Either way, I want to know if my program works on mice, and if you are new, you will do nicely as another subject. If you have not been properly conditioned we will see that it is done."

Dr. Somogyi went to the recorder, turned up the volume, and placed it directly in front of Seymour's cage. "OK, mouse, we will find out if your brain is as remarkable as the rest of your body appears to be." After a few minutes, satisfied that the mouse was fixated on the video, he left the room.

Seymour was indeed watching the recording, but he was having no part of it. He had made it successfully through the earlier sessions with only small effect, and he felt he could survive more of this brainwashing.

But Dr. Somogyi was not to be fooled. He had learned from the attendant that this was a stray mouse that Evans caught last night, not one of the mice in the program. Exasperated that Evans had failed to advise him immediately, he knew that it was only because he himself recognized that this mouse was different that he was able to keep the program and the experiments from being contaminated. He returned to Seymour's cage.

Thinking out loud, with no idea that this mouse understood every word he said, Dr. Somogyi murmured, "Well, mouse, since you were not in the program from the start, we have not had the benefit of a full examination and we have no baseline on you. Now we must put you through the indoctrination program that I designed for new participants. I am pleased that you are big and strong for a mouse, because you will need your strength. Rest now; I will return shortly." And he continued on his rounds, checking the other animals.

Once again, Seymour had a decision to make. He could try to escape now, while he had the chance, or wait to see exactly what Dr. Somogyi was up to. Having heard the doctor's ominous remarks, leaving was a very attractive alternative. But he knew that if there was any possibility of finding out more about the animal testing and, even more importantly, Attila Dome, this was the place to do it. Yes, it would put him in danger, but seeing all the other animals being held captive here, and remembering what was being done to Melissa and the mice back at Mrs. Bennett's house, and what harm Attila Dome could do, his sense of responsibility got the better of him. He had no choice but to stay where he was and deal with it, come what may.

Chapter 14

Seymour Makes a Mistake

In retrospect, Seymour's decision to stay may have been the wrong one. He watched Dr. Somogyi and Ricky as they wheeled a cart carrying several vials of medicine and electronic machines with a host of wires connecting them into the room. He had seen similar carts on medical and hospital television shows at Mr. Saunders's house, but never up close. When they stopped in front of his cage and he understood that all this was meant for him, he knew he should run for his life. But before he could move an inch, Dr. Somogyi sprayed him with some sort of mist. His vision suddenly darkened, his body collapsed, and as he fell to the floor of the cage, his mind went blank.

Seymour had no idea how long he had been unconscious, but when he awoke he was lying on the cart with wires attached to his chest and paws. He was unable to move his head: it was held down, as were his arms and legs, taped to the table. The wires led to one of the machines, and he was able to shift his eyes just enough to see on the monitor a series of blinking numbers that he understood were his vital signs. He also sensed a metal plate under his body. He felt terribly alone, helpless and fearful; a very new experience for him. How could he have allowed this to happen? Why hadn't he left when he had the chance? It dawned on him that now he might not be able to help himself, let alone Melissa or any of these animals. And what about alerting the officials about Attila Dome? Had he missed his chance?

Just then he could feel someone attaching wires to his scalp and ears. These wires were also connected to a machine. Although he could not move much, he was able to catch sight of another mouse lying alongside him on the cart, similarly wired. What, he wondered, was going on here? Why two of us? He looked up and saw Dr. Somogyi peering down at him.

"All right, mouse, let's see what's in your brain, and how robust your body is before we begin your indoctrination, shall we?" And with that he turned on one of the monitors. Seymour glimpsed the machine out of the corner of his eyes. Lines and numbers appeared. Somogyi watched them as well and said something to Ricky, who promptly adjusted the wires on Seymour's head.

"That's better," murmured Dr. Somogyi. "We are getting a good reading on this one." Then he cleared his throat and said, "At 3:30 PM on Tuesday, let the record show that, regarding Mouse 23, the new larger male mouse, its breathing and heart rate are a bit elevated for a mouse, but I believe that the trauma of the knockout spray we administered, and being taped to the table, may well account for these readings. Let us now see how Mouse 17 is doing."

Dr. Somogyi and the attendant moved to watch the readings of the other mouse. After a few moments he heard Somogyi say, "Mouse 17's readings appear stable and are within normal bounds. For the record, this mouse has been in the program for 21 days."

While the two men were watching Mouse 17, Seymour strained at his bonds, trying to free himself, but he could not move his arms, legs or head even a centimeter. He focused and held his breath and, gathering all his strength, attempted to rise. It was useless: he could not budge the tapes that held him. He lay there waiting for whatever Dr. Somogyi had planned. He didn't have to wait long.

"Ricky, compare Mouse 23 with Mouse 17, and tell me what you see," said Dr. Somogyi.

"Doctor," Ricky replied, "Mouse 23 reads heart rate 101, respiration 80. Mouse 17's heart rate is 90 and respiration 62."

"That's fine," Dr. Somogyi said. "Turn on the audio."

Seymour heard the voice say the pledge, "Cats are good; cats are the best; cats never eat mice," over and over for several minutes.

"Compare the two again," Dr. Somogyi ordered.

"Doctor, Mouse 23's heart rate reads 128, and the respiration is 96. Mouse 17's heart rate is 78 and the respiration is 57."

"Yes, what we have here is classic," crowed Dr. Somogyi. "This means my program is working! Mouse 17 accepts the pledge, but Mouse 23 is resisting it." Hearing the Doctor, Seymour thought that phrase might be the trigger for mice becoming cats. Somogyi continued. "Mouse 17 feels better about hearing the familiar words, so the body relaxes. Our desensitization has changed him. On the other hand, this larger mouse is resisting the pledge and is struggling inside. And look at him; he is even struggling to get free. He knows that cats are his enemy, and he cannot believe those words. He knows that they are against his very nature, against all his knowledge and experience. So, we must change him. Get me the Scopolamine, and wire him for shock."

The next thing Seymour knew, the doctor was swabbing some lotion on his body, then a needle was inserted and he felt a warm fluid enter his body. In a minute or two, he felt calmer. The attendant turned the audio on again. Seymour heard the familiar voice that spoke the pledge, but this time it brought a different message. "Calm down, Brother Mouse, calm down. Do not resist, you will be fine. You are in a laboratory under the care of one of the finest doctors in the world. You will not be hurt, you will be cured of any illness that you might have, and relieved of any fears. You will be a better mouse than ever. That is why you are here."

Despite his apprehension, Seymour was feeling calmer when suddenly a blinding shock ran through his body, almost lifting him off the table. He tried to control himself, but the terrible jolt and pain caused him to scream loud and long. When he had control of his senses again, he remembered what Dr. DeStefano had told him about the Monarch

"Come back here, you little rat!"

Program. So he knew that what had hit him was electricity, but how much of this could his body withstand? He hoped that he had not spoken any English words in his screams.

Then the voice on the recorder started again. "Please Brother, do not cry, this treatment will help you and make you a better mouse. Please listen to me. There is nothing to be afraid of. There are no cats here, nothing to harm you. The doctor and his aide are here to help you to be a more accepting and wise mouse, a mouse that knows that he will be the best mouse in the world. You will come to see and understand that other animals, such as cats, are not here in the world to harm us. They are superior to mice, yes, I know it may be hard for you to believe it, but they are. But, and this is why you are here, you can become a cat yourself. Yes, you can. After just a few days of this training, you will understand that not only are cats harmless to mice, you will see yourself as a cat. You will in fact join them and become a cat." Then the shock exploded through his body again and Seymour passed out.

When he awoke, he found himself back in his cage and, checking the window behind the cages, he saw that there was still some daylight left. Seymour wondered how sound he was. He flexed his muscles, clenched his paws, felt his arms, legs and body, and checked his memory. Considering all he had been through, he felt well enough and only had a slight headache. He knew that the mouse he had been on the table with was in the next cage, so he called to him in mouse speak. "Mouse, are you still with us? Mouse 17, can you hear me? Are you still a mouse, or are you now a cat? I hope you remain a mouse, you are a fine mouse." There was no movement from the mouse, nor was there an answer.

The audio was on again in front of his cage, and he could see Dr. Somogyi making his rounds, writing notes about each animal on his clipboard. As the doctor neared his cage, he said, "So, Mouse 23, how are we doing? I think we are off to a good start, don't you? In a while you will make a very good cat. Let me get a better look at you."

Somogyi moved the clipboard to his left hand and unlocked the door to the cage with his right. He reached in to pick up Seymour, but Seymour was now determined to get out. He had no idea what

Somogyi next had in mind, but instinct told him he had seen enough and undergone enough treatment. He backed further into the cage and grabbed for his sack, but Somogyi was quick and reached in further. "Come here, you elusive creature," he growled. "I need to see you closer."

Just then the mouse in the next cage began to scream. "Eeeek! Eeeek!" Dr. Somogyi, distracted by the noise, turned and looked at the mouse. "What is wrong with you, Mouse 17," he scoffed, but the mouse kept up his squealing, "Eeeek! Eeeek!" Taking advantage of the moment, Seymour grabbed hold of his sack and bit the scientist's hand as hard as he could. He ran out the open cage door and climbed up on top of his cage. From there he leaped on to the cage next to his, yelled a thank you to Mouse 17, and ran across cages and counter tops to the still partially open window.

Dr. Somogyi screamed in pain and threw his clipboard at Seymour, the papers flying in the air all around him. "Come back here, you little rat!" he howled, holding his bleeding hand. "Someone, Ricky, get in here now!" he shouted. "Mouse 23 is out and getting away!"

Ricky came in fast and the two of them ran to the window, searching for Seymour as they went. But Seymour had made good his escape and was already half way down the side of the building with his sack. He saw the window fly open all the way and the two men hanging out, yelling and pointing at him. The doctor, still holding his bitten hand, shouted to two pedestrians passing by. "Stop that mouse! Stop that rat! He is rabid! Kill him! Don't let him get away!"

The two people looked up at the building, saw the men in the window, but they had no idea what, or why, they were yelling. If they had known what to look for they might have spied Seymour, who was right behind them on the ground, hugging the building side of the sidewalk, by this time half way down the block and heading for his bus. "There he goes," Dr. Somogyi screeched. "Get that mouse! Stop that rat! He is rabid and must be caught and killed. Stop him! I am a doctor!" Then he turned on the unfortunate attendant Ricky. "You! Go down there and get him or kill him. Now!"

This was New York City, where people generally mind their own business and where eccentric behavior is commonplace, so the two pedestrians looked up at Somogyi again, then at each other, shrugged their shoulders and continued on their way. Whatever was going on, it was not their problem. And seeing mice or rats in New York City? Ho hum.

Chapter 15

Seymour Makes Some Phone Calls

Ricky reached street level and ran in the direction that Seymour was heading, east to Amsterdam Avenue. But Seymour was already there and in his bus. He started it up and swung into the traffic, then sped north on Amsterdam Avenue away from the laboratory.

He knew he had to call the animal rights people, and the New York City police, but before that, he really had to find out whether Attila Dome was in fact more than just an idea in Dr. Dempsey's head. Also, who was the other person, Enrico Gonzalez? The NYPD could check with the FBI and the CIA, but he had an idea that he thought might give him the information he needed on these scientists more quickly.

Seymour had recently returned from Spain, where he had helped solve an important case for the Spanish government involving French citizens who had stolen extremely valuable property from Spanish wine growers. Now, it was he who needed help so he thought he would start there. He pulled over to the curb, grabbed his iPhone, looked up contacts and recent numbers and dialed Manuel Maria Salinas's number in Jerez de la Frontera. Checking the time difference mentally, he realized it was very late in the evening in Spain and he hoped his call would be answered. After several rings, he was dismayed to hear Salinas's voice on the answering machine. Seymour had begun his message when he heard a familiar voice on the other end.

"Seymour, I trust? I saw the calling number and knew immediately who it was," said Salinas in English. "How are you and what can I do for you, my friend?" Señor Salinas had been Seymour's primary contact in the Spanish case, and they knew each other well. Seymour apologized for the late call and need for urgency, but he told Señor Salinas that time was of the essence. So, skipping the pleasantries, he quickly filled him in on the reason for the call. He explained about the animals, the brainwashing and torture at the lab, and the names of the people behind it, Dr. Peter Dempsey, Enrico Gonzalez and Dr. Laszlo Somogyi, and Attila Dome. He told Señor Salinas that he was in his bus, and afraid that the lab personnel might get away if he did not return to the lab in a few minutes. He asked Señor Salinas if he still had contacts in the Spanish National Police. Fortunately, Señor Salinas confirmed that he had.

"Señor Salinas, could you pass on those three names as well as the term "Attila Dome" to them right away? Please inform them there might be international implications in this matter and we need to know the result immediately as I am about to call the police. Also, could you ask them to check with the French National Police and INTERPOL, as perhaps they have information linking those names with animals or mind control."

Seymour spent a few more moments spelling out the names and again stressed the urgency of the matter. Señor Salinas said he would get right on it and let Seymour know promptly if he was able to learn anything that would help.

After signing off with Salinas, Seymour had another idea. What better way to expose these scientists' terrible work than to arrange a raid accompanied by top-notch media coverage? But first things first: newspapers and television stations would not prosecute the criminal; that was a job for local law enforcement. Still pulled over on Amsterdam Avenue, he called the office of Kevin Reilly, New York City's Police Commissioner. From time to time over the years, Seymour had been instrumental in solving a variety of cases in New York City that had eluded the city's police. He was well acquainted with Commissioner Reilly and the department, so he expected to receive some favorable treatment. When the switchboard operator learned who it was on the phone, he put the call straight through.

"Well, Seymour," said Commissioner Reilly upon answering. "It's good to hear from you. How have you been?"

"Mostly fine, Commissioner, how about you? Are things going well in New York?"

"They are good enough, Seymour. The crime rate is down, the mayor is a bit of a problem as always, but things could be worse. What's up? What can I do for you?"

"I am on the upper West Side on 114th street," said Seymour, "and there is something going on here that you ought to know about. I am a few blocks away from a laboratory at Columbia University in which dozens of animals are being kept in cages, which must be in violation of the health codes and animal cruelty laws. This is not a normal animal care facility in any way. In fact, it is clear that many of these animals are being tortured in a new and troublesome manner. I think this is something that the police need to be involved in."

"Whoa, Seymour, slow down. Did you say that this activity is going on right now, and here in New York?"

"Yes, Commissioner, I just came from the laboratory. It is right here in Manhattan."

"Seymour, you also said it was on Columbia University property, did you not?"

"I believe the building where the animals are being kept also houses a laboratory which is shared with Columbia. But I am not sure of the ownership."

"The reason I ask is that universities do have a large number of laboratories in their Biology, Chemistry, Engineering, and Physics Departments. Even though Columbia does not have a Veterinary School, Columbia's College of Physicians and Surgeons, their medical school, may well engage in animal testing. So it's not uncommon for a university to have laboratories with animals in them. Nor is it against the law."

"I am aware of that, Commissioner," said Seymour, "but these animals are being brainwashed and tortured. Of that I am certain. I was a victim there myself, locked in a cage, given drugs and electric shock, and I just escaped a few minutes ago. There appear to be well over a hundred animals of many species being kept there. I can't believe that they are connected with any legitimate university departmental purpose."

"I am appalled at what you just told me, Seymour. However, we are on uncertain legal ground here," said the chief. "I myself went to Columbia, to their Law School. It is one of the foremost universities in the country, and has a superb reputation for the manner in which they run their programs. And, although I am not an expert in this field, I do not think that brainwashing or thought control with animals is against the law in the U.S. If we were to storm in there and make arrests, we, the police department, and the City of New York could be held liable for false arrest and sued for a lot of money. So Seymour, what exactly is it that you would have me do?"

"Commissioner," said Seymour. "I understand all you have said, and I rely upon your judgment and counsel. I appreciate that this is one of the finest schools in the world. However, I have to believe that the administration of Columbia, their faculty, and their Board of Trustees know nothing of what is going on in this lab. Even if there are no specific laws being broken regarding brainwashing per se, the treatment of animals in this manner, including torture, is simply wrong. And I believe the animal brainwashing is only one step in a program they call The Attila Dome, whose ultimate goal is to extend mind control to humans. I have reached out to one of my contacts in Europe to see if he can shed some light on this matter as well, since there may well be international interest in this matter. And, I was told that brainwashing may or not, be against the law, but torture most certainly is in all our 50 states. Commissioner, we will be doing the animals, the university, our government and perhaps others a huge favor if we can halt these experiments now and hold the scientists accountable. Might I persuade you to join me so you can see for yourself what I have uncovered?"

Commissioner Reilly said nothing for a while. Finally, he spoke. "Seymour, I trust you too much not to say yes to your request. I will contact the local precinct and have them on standby. And, even though I have a law degree, would you mind if I bring along someone from our legal department who also acts as the primary liaison for the NYPD with the EU countries? I am also thinking that people from the ASPCA would be valuable. That is an organization we both respect. Their people could be witnesses to what is going on, and they could handle the animals you say are there. What do you think?"

"That is fine Commissioner, it is exactly what is needed," Seymour said with relief. "The address of the building is 628 West 114th Street. The sign says Intercultural Resource Center, but the lab I am referring to, the East Coast Laboratory, is inside. Believe me, it is no 'cultural center'."

"OK, Seymour, you wait there. I will call our legal staff representative, contact the ASPCA, and explain the situation to both of them. My men and I should be there within the hour."

Chapter 16

Help Arrives

Seymour knew he had some time before the animal rights people and the New York City police would arrive, so he turned his thoughts to a plan to generate media coverage that would expose these scientists' nefarious work by shedding light on their operation. He felt that a combination of television and newspaper stories would prove a great front-page story for their viewers and readers, and it would also be an irresistible topic for the talk radio stations. Add to the story some photo shots and videos, it would expose Dr. Somogyi and Dr. Dempsey's animal brainwashing experiments to millions in the greater New York region. It could also uncover Dempsey's and Gonzalez's heinous Attila Dome plan, a plan which might soon involve human beings with unimaginable consequences.

He Googled some of the key telephone numbers he needed and added them to his directory. He then called the New York affiliates of the major TV networks, NBC, CBS, Fox and ABC, and outlined what was going on. With the same introduction he called the local newspapers, such as the New York Times, the Daily News, and the New York Post. Finally, he alerted the leading New York radio news and talk stations, WCBS, WOR, WINS, and WNYC, the National Public Radio station in New York. Seymour explained who he was, told them what was going on, and provided the address of the lab. All those he spoke with were skeptical at first, but the story sounded bizarre enough, and interesting enough, that Seymour felt they would follow up. No stranger to publicity, he knew that news organizations always wanted to be first with a story, so he calculated that his calls would produce some results, and fast.

Seymour moved his bus a bit closer to the East Coast Laboratory and waited for a call from Señor Salinas. After forty-five minutes, he saw the police SWAT team arrive with sirens blaring and lights flashing, and just then his phone rang. It was Salinas. As he reached for his iPhone he could see that right on the heels of the police were several TV crews, and they soon had their cameras rolling. He also spotted a van with ASPCA lettering on the driver's door, pulling up just behind the police. Realizing that he was running out of time, he decided to take the call but make it brief.

"Seymour," said Señor Salinas, "it is very interesting what I have learned. First, we have no record of Dr. Somogyi's travelling to Europe in the last several years. There are records about his education and early career in Romania, and I will get back to that in a moment. But it seems that your Dr. Dempsey arrived in Amsterdam, Netherlands a few weeks ago and began buying animals as fast as he could, any and all he could find. What alerted the authorities there was his interest in wild animals as well as domestic; he was not concerned where he got them, and money seemed no object. The police alerted the People for the Ethical Treatment of Animals (PETA) in the Netherlands and along with them visited Dr. Dempsey in his new lab. There they found the same type of arrangement as you described there in New York. He had videos and electrical shock equipment and they actually caught him with animals strapped to a table, wired to machines and howling in pain. He was arrested, and he is now trying to contact his attorneys to get him out of jail."

"Señor Salinas," said Seymour, "I cannot thank you enough for your prompt response. I will pass this on to our police here, and I am sure they will be in touch."

"Wait, Seymour, there is more," said Salinas. "It is about this Enrico Gonzalez. INTERPOL is very interested in him and the Attila Dome project. They found several references to that phrase, extending back some years. Nothing in the immediate past, but Dr. Somogyi was mentioned as doing the seminal work in mind control with animals and laying the foundation for similar measures in humans. And those four stages you cited showed up prominently in connection with Gonzalez and Dempsey. As I said, INTERPOL in the Netherlands already has Dr. Dempsey in custody, and they have reason to believe that Gonzalez is in the United States. They would very much like to speak with him, if he can be found."

Seymour earnestly thanked Señor Salinas, and assured him that he would pass on the information to the police and follow up with him as soon as things quieted down on his end.

Seymour got out of his bus and waved to the Commissioner, who had two others with him. The Commissioner said a quick hello to Seymour and introduced him first to Dr. Angela Nevins. He explained that she was the head of the ASPCA's Anti-Cruelty Group in New York and that they were very interested in stopping just this sort of criminal activity. She had brought a dozen members of her staff along to help. Seymour was grateful for their assistance and said he hoped they could rescue all the animals here and place them in better surroundings.

The Commissioner then introduced the Assistant Deputy Commissioner of Legal Matters for the City, Pietro Accorsi, and explained that he was here to ensure that all activities were carried out in the proper manner so as to avoid legal challenges. The Deputy would also handle international tie-ins, if there were any. Seymour confirmed that there were some matters that would need co-ordination and gave Mr. Accorsi a thumbnail sketch of his talk with Salinas. The formalities completed, Seymour begged off and explained that right now he had another job to complete.

He ran to the front of the building just as the SWAT team was forming. The men were gathering near a Mobile Command Center vehicle that had pulled up, and were putting on their Kevlar jackets and

"... *the SWAT team drew their weapons* ..."

gas masks. Seymour found and introduced himself to the officer in charge, a Sgt. Burns. The team was from the 24th precinct, Burns explained, and this was their territory. Burns looked hard at Seymour, and said that he had heard stories of a mouse that had assisted the New York and New Jersey police in the past, but had never quite believed them. Seymour stood tall, looked Burns in the eye and said yes, he was that mouse. The very surprised sergeant shook his paw and said he was delighted to meet him.

Seymour asked if they were comfortable having him share the lead on this operation, and after checking with Commissioner Reilly, Sgt. Burns confirmed that they were. Seymour called Dr. Nevins and her team over to join the group. Gathering the SWAT and ASPCA teams around him, he told them who he was and why both the police and the ASPCA had been called in. He explained that there was an animal laboratory in the building, and that unlawful experiments, including torture and brainwashing, were being conducted there. He told them that he had been inside the lab just an hour or so ago, and there were approximately one hundred animals in cages, many of them wild, which was why the ASPCA people had been called in.

Sgt. Burns asked, "Seymour, how many people are inside? And do you know if there are weapons or hazardous materials to deal with?" Seymour replied that he believed that there were several animal attendants and scientists inside, but he had never seen any weapons. As to other materials and substances, there were some toxic and perhaps illicit drugs being used, and he could not be 100% sure that there were no other harmful substances inside. Burns said that's why the SWAT team was involved, as they had to be prepared for all situations, including the possibility that they might meet resistance from the people running the laboratory.

When the teams were ready, Seymour described what he knew of the interior layout, how many people he had seen inside, and where they might be located. Burns checked his men, asked if they were ready to go. Given the thumbs up, the SWAT team drew their weapons, and they were off, with Seymour leading the way. The ASPCA people remained at the front of the building until it was pronounced safe for them, and the media crowd was right on their heels.

Just as Seymour charged into the building he glanced down 113th Street and spotted Ricky walking toward them. Suddenly noticing the police and media, and all the bright lights, Ricky stopped in his tracks, turned on his heel and strode quickly away, whipping off his white lab coat and stuffing it into a trash bin as he went.

Sgt. Burns and his men followed Seymour through the door and up the stairs. As they advanced, the media people had their cameras rolling, capturing the mouse and the police charging into the building. Seymour had seen that the doors to the cage rooms were usually unlocked, and there was no reason for the attendants to expect trouble, so he expected they would have fairly easy access to the animals. But now, with all this activity, he was not so sure. Dr. Somogyi had no way of knowing that Seymour had called the authorities, but he was certainly aware of the illicit nature of this dastardly business, and had to notice the police sirens and flashing lights in front of the building. If he was feeling like a cornered rat, what might he do?

Chapter 17

Somogyi Arrested

Seymour had told the police that the third floor was where the animals were kept, so they were able to check and clear the empty offices of the first and second floors quickly. In the lead on the stairs nearing the third floor, Seymour had his eyes glued on the corridor ahead. The police followed in single file, taking a step at a time and using hand signals, not knowing who or what they would find. They all reached the top and filed into the corridor. Here, Sgt. Burns asked Seymour to move out of the way and let them lead; they were trained on how to enter a room where there might be hostiles. On the count of three, the SWAT team charged into the first room and surprised two lab technicians who were gathering lab records and notes and feeding them into a paper shredder. Seymour could see that these records were not from the desk in the office, the ones he was most concerned about. The technicians were quickly taken into custody. The police checked the rooms where the animals were held and declared them safe for Dr. Nevins and her team. The ASPCA team took charge of the cages and the animals were accepted into their custody. As they went from room to room, Seymour asked the police to confiscate all the brainwashing videotapes.

Down on the street, as was normal in any city, crowds were gathering to witness the commotion, drawn by squad cars and TV cameras.

The spectators wondered what was going on as rescuers brought out the animals, specie after specie, and placed them in ASPCA vans. During all this, the TV cameras were rolling, and it was all caught on video. It was a fantastic human-interest story, and the New York reporters and camera crews knew that this would make great headlines in the morning. They would have evidence of the cages, the dazed animals, and they knew that no one ever wanted to see animals abused.

Seymour, though, wanted the TV crews that were in the lab to follow the police and film the frantic technicians trying to destroy the written evidence of brainwashing and all that went with the purpose of the lab. They took pictures of the cages, the machines and videos and instruments and wires and vials of medicines, of the metal tables with pieces of tape where the animals had been restrained and tortured. It presented a devastating image of the cruel acts that had transpired there.

And the cameras were rolling when Dr. Somogyi was found in Dr. Dempsey's office, hastily grabbing his notes from his desk and placing them into a briefcase. Seymour noted that the document explaining the Attila Dome was among those he shoved in the briefcase, and saw one of the SWAT team take it away from Somogyi and hand it to Sgt. Burns.

Also caught on camera was the scene when Dr. Somogyi was handcuffed and led out of the building. Coming out the front door, he happened to see Seymour amidst the ASPCA workers. Somogyi was enraged and screamed at Seymour, looking right at him, "You! It was you, Mouse 23, you did this to me! You will pay for this. I will get you, and I will see you destroyed!"

If Dr. Somogyi wasn't already mad enough, he was beside himself when Sgt. Burns told him that he was being arrested for cruelty under Section 353 of the New York Penal Code, and read him his Miranda rights there on the front steps.

"You have no authority here," Somogyi sputtered. "I have done nothing wrong! What right has anyone to enter this laboratory uninvited? This is private property. These were my scientific experiments and now you people have ruined years of my work. No animal was killed. No animal was even hurt! Where is your search warrant?" Sgt. Burns explained that they did not need a search warrant in this instance because a crime was in the process of being committed.

On all these serious matters, neither Seymour nor Sgt. Burns wanted to challenge Dr. Somogyi right then and there. He would get his day in court. There was a mountain of evidence against him, and Seymour himself would certainly be able to testify on a first hand basis that animals did get hurt while in the evil scientist's program, he having been one of them. But he knew that there would be time for that later.

But Dr. Somogyi would not keep quiet. "What crime? Where is your lawful subpoena to confiscate my papers?" he demanded. Again, Sgt. Burns told him they did not need a subpoena in this case, as the papers were evidence gathered at the scene of a crime, and would be passed on to the District Attorney. "Well," Somogyi roared, "you will hear from my lawyers within the hour. Everyone here is going to be sued, for millions. I am outraged. I am a doctor. These are my patients!"

The police asked him to come with them and they walked him down the stairs and into a police vehicle. As they emerged from the building, the newspaper reporters and camera crews met them with a blinding barrage of flash bulbs, spotlights, and TV cameras. They watched as the disgraced man in the white coat was stuffed into the back seat of a police cruiser. They could see that Dr. Somogyi, so irate as he was being hauled off to jail, was not making a lot of sense. Some people in the crowd swore they heard the doctor babbling about a large mouse that had escaped his program and jumped out the window, that this mouse was a spy for his enemies who were plotting against him. "I did the research! All the work on animals, it was my work, and now it is stolen due to that mouse. Others will take credit, but it was mine!" Incredible, they thought, and it certainly made for good theater.

Seymour met again with Commissioner Reilly, Mr. Accorsi, and Dr. Nevins, who were in between interviews with the press, and thanked them once more. He related what he knew about Dempsey in Amsterdam, the lab there and the PETA connection as well as the searches of databases by INTERPOL on Somogyi, Dempsey and

Gonzalez, and the hits they got. By then the cameras had turned to them. He knew that the New York City police and the ASPCA deserved good publicity, and this opportunity to talk to the people of New York was not to be missed. Seymour, however, declined to be interviewed by the press, saying his contribution was to alert the police and the ASPCA, and that they were the heroes here today, not he. He was just happy to see the helpless animals now in good hands.

Before he left the scene, and being ever careful, Seymour went back to the third floor and made sure there were no tools left in the cage where he had been kept. He had done nothing wrong in escaping, but he did not want to have to explain to anyone how a small Swiss Army knife had found its way into one of the cages. Then he went into Dr. Dempsey's office to make sure that the manila envelope had indeed been retrieved from the file cabinet by the authorities. When he was satisfied that there was nothing of importance left behind, he went back down to the street.

Standing outside the building and as far away from the cameras as he could, Seymour met with Sgt. Burns and thanked him and his men for a job well done. He asked if there was a chance he could take a look at Dr. Somogyi's briefcase before it was taken away with the other evidence. Sgt. Burns said that, in keeping with the chain of custody laws, he and his men had to keep all evidence secure until it was delivered to the District Attorney, but there was no reason why Seymour couldn't look at it. He called over one of the SWAT team who opened the briefcase, and there, right on top of a pile of other papers, Seymour could see the envelope. He told the sergeant that it was imperative that Commissioner Reilly and Mr. Accorsi see that particular piece of evidence, as it had international implications. After assuring Seymour that he would take care of that personally, Sgt. Burns asked him to stop by at their precinct before he left the area and give his statement about what he learned about the East Coast Laboratory. Seymour said of course, he would be right there.

Retrieving his bus, Seymour drove to the precinct headquarters and made his report. He stated that when he saw what was happening to Melissa, he consulted Mr. Saunders, who introduced him to Dr. DeStefano at Rutgers, an expert on brainwashing and mind control. That he followed Melissa to Mrs. Bennett's house, and saw the letters from the East Coast Laboratory and Dr. Dempsey's name there. That he had located the lab on 113th Street, and that he had entered the lab through an open window and witnessed the animals being held in cages. He explained that he felt he had to assist them as they were being held against their will and being forced to act against their nature while being indoctrinated by a constant barrage of messages. He told how he himself had been caught, strapped down, drugged, and given electric shock. That he managed to search the office, find the envelope, make good his escape, and then call the police as soon as he was able. The police, he said, responded swiftly and brought in the ASPCA. Seymour also said there could be international connections to this case. He admitted that it was he who had called the media to get the whole story on record.

After hearing Seymour's recount of events, the police were more than satisfied with his statement, and they applauded him for his bravery while in captivity. When they were finished, he quietly got in his school bus and drove back home.

When he arrived at the barn, he made sure all was well with the mice, especially Melissa. Tomorrow, he vowed, he would begin her deprogramming therapy. As he turned to head to his own bed, his phone rang and he saw it was Señor Salinas.

Chapter 18

Back at the Barn

Salinas apologized for the late hour, and said if Seymour had a few minutes, he was calling not only to find out how things went with the raid on the laboratory but to relate a few other details there had been no time for in their earlier conversation. Seymour gave Salinas the high points of the raid, the capture of Dr. Somogyi and the release of the animals, then told him to please go ahead with some of the other details.

"Well, that is splendid work, Seymour, for sure," said Salinas. He went on. "So, regarding the Attila Dome project, it seems that INTERPOL cannot find any evidence that Dr. Somogyi had any part in that scheme, other than the fact that it may be based on his earlier research at the Polytechnia in Bucharest. The local INTERPOL branch there in Bucharest has had no contact or interest in Somogyi for over thirty years. They also checked with the Romanian Police, who said the same. So, he may be a cruel scientist operating outside the law with the lab, but he is not to their knowledge directly part of the Attila Dome initiative.

"However, here is where it gets interesting. Outside Bucharest lies the small town of Ramnicu Valcea, a cybercrime hot spot, also known to police across Europe as Hackerville Central. In their database, INTERPOL found quite a few entries for an Enrico Gonzalez.

Originally from my country, he is apparently quite a "cybercriminal". He loved the Internet, and used it in Spain to extort money from a variety of people. But he was not very proficient at covering his tracks, so he was constantly hounded by the police. He moved from Madrid to Ramnicu Valcea some ten years ago to learn from the best hackers, and he was soon able to break into the accounts of people of means, many of them Americans. His specialty was diverting funds into accounts he set up himself. Gonzalez became so good at his trade that he moved to the U.S. and set up his operation there. And here's the connection: one of the people he swindled was our Dr. Dempsey, who in short order found himself almost destitute. While going through Dempsey's computer files, Gonzalez must have learned that he was a specialist in mind control and brainwashing, and that he wanted to continue Dr. Somogyi's controversial work to see whether it would be transferrable to human beings.

"This apparently intrigued Gonzalez and his criminal mind. He must have been able to see that if he could bring this off, and control the minds of humans, he could have a fleet of people in countries all over the world doing whatever he desired.

"Which brings us to seeking help from the FBI. From what the Romanian Police were able to detect, the two somehow got together and formed an unholy alliance. Using the funds Gonzalez could steal, they now had the financial means that Dempsey so desperately needed. Here was a marriage, but one surely not made in heaven."

"But why," Seymour asked out loud, "don't we know anything about Gonzalez here in New York, other than finding his name on the Attila Dome note we found in Dr. Dempsey's file cabinet?"

"I don't really know," Salinas responded. "Let me look at my notes to see if I left anything out. Hmmm," he mused. "Ricky was born and lived in Madrid, got into trouble and moved to Romania where he met the premier hackers, and..."

"Wait," interrupted Seymour. "Did you just call Gonzalez, Ricky?"

"Yes, Seymour, Ricky is short for Enrico. He appears in the database as Enrico 'Ricky' Gonzalez."

"That's it, Señor Salinas!" Seymour exclaimed excitedly. "Ricky was the name of the attendant in the lab. And he had a Spanish accent! He must have been working with Dempsey all along, spying on Dr. Somogyi in order to learn all he could about animal brainwashing. The two of them were using Dr. Somogyi, and he never knew it. Whether or not that will help him with the authorities, I don't know, but it puts Enrico Gonzalez right here in the lab. He is in the wind now; I saw him running away down 113th Street just as the SWAT team was heading into the building. He may be hard to find, but we must share what we now know with the authorities.

"Señor Salinas," Seymour continued, "you have turned into an outstanding sleuth. Thank you for tracking down this vital information. I am sure that you will be hearing from Pietro Accorsi at the NYPD. The facts you have provided will help put these men in jail, and keep them there for a very long time."

"I'm more than happy to help, Seymour," said Salinas. "Without your assistance over here, the French vintners would be growing our grapes and making our Sherry. We will always be in your debt."

In the morning, Seymour met with Mr. Saunders and they jointly called Dr. DeStefano, who had already heard about the raid on the lab on the morning news. Seymour told them about the envelope outlining the Attila Dome project, and the parts that Dempsey and Gonzalez played. They all agreed that it was not for public knowledge at this point, better in the hands of the FBI or the CIA, where the NYC police had most likely delivered it. Dr. DeStefano was relieved to learn that Dr. Dempsey was not at Rutgers, but in an Amsterdam jail where he belonged.

Busting up the "Animal Lab from Hell" was the lead story on television, radio, and the newspapers for several days. Mr. Saunders was especially proud of how Seymour had cracked the case, using his skills, his courage and his sense of duty and honor by staying in the cage until he was certain that Somogyi, Dempsey and Gonzalez were the team behind the crimes. Seymour told him of his own ordeal while captured, and that Dr. DeStefano had assured him that he would most likely have

"… Seymour guided Melissa back to her normal sweet self."

little or no after effects of the Scopolamine or shock treatment, since he had been subjected to them only the one time.

Also in the news was a statement from a public relations spokesperson for Columbia University, admitting that the East Coast Laboratory did jointly sponsor some research with Columbia, but they claimed it was in the nature of ensuring safer marine transportation, nothing to do with animals. They were outraged at this unlawful use of their facilities, trusted that Dr. Somogyi would be brought to justice, and hoped that this smear on their reputation had been removed.

Footage of Dr. Somogyi heading to jail was especially gratifying to watch, and the front page of the New York Post had a picture of Somogyi being put into the police cruiser with the caption, "Evil Scientist behind Animal Brainwashing and Torture." But equally as pleasing to Seymour and Mr. Saunders was a picture on the front page of The Daily News: Seymour leading the police up the steps to the lab with the caption, "Don't Mess with this Mouse!"

After reading the stories in the papers and watching the TV reports, Seymour went to the barn and met with Melissa. Because she had been in the program for quite a while, he was anxious to begin the deprogramming protocol that Dr. DeStefano had prescribed. Over the next several weeks they worked together on recovery, taking it slowly as Seymour guided Melissa back to her normal sweet self. Gently giving her the real facts about cats, and showing her with words and deeds what fine little animals mice were, Seymour was relieved to see that they had gotten to her in time.

Dr. Dempsey was still in the Netherlands, and so Seymour never learned how he met Mrs. Bennett. However that vile partnership began, either Dempsey or Somogyi must have discovered what an easy target the poor woman was to brainwash and control, and used her for their program.

The cat episode was soon in the past for Melissa. Seymour was pleased when he came upon her running and playing silly games with the other mice, teasing them and laughing at their antics. Melissa even went a step further, and checked in frequently with all her little siblings and cousins, making sure they were happy, and feeling loved and appreciated.

But from time to time Seymour did see Mrs. Bennett on her hands and knees in the grass in her back yard, trying to catch a bird with her mouth. Seymour really didn't think it was his job to try and deprogram her. Let her be a cat if that's what made her happy.

End

Acknowledgements

Seymour was born in stories told to my children, Jenni, Matt, and Sam, as well as my nephews Patrick, Bryan, and Christopher, and grandchildren Alex, Gillie, Ben, Zack, Maddie, Zoe and Will. Thanks for listening, guys.

There are many people who have helped bring Seymour to life, and I would like to express my appreciation to them. First and foremost is my wife, Heather. She knows Seymour as well as I do, and has been through the countless re-writes and edits of this manuscript. Her resolve in turning my well-intentioned sentences into readable English is amazing. My son Sam also helped with edits and added a few twists to the plot to heighten the suspense. Mistakes, however, if any, are entirely mine.

And a special thank you goes to Dennis Yap for his truly wonderful illustrations.

I also want to thank members of the New Jersey Children's Writers Guild, headed by Jack and Sheila Wright, and the Bridgewater Critique Group who helped guide me through the process of writing fiction. Their patience, suggestions and support have helped me immensely.

Made in the USA
Middletown, DE
26 March 2016